THE SECOND HOUSE

When Liza Durant is saved from drowning by Jeffrey Forrest, she little realizes how much it will change her life. Jeffrey is the heir to the old manor La Deuxieme, the 'second house'. Within days he proposes to Liza, who agrees to visit him at his country home. A series of accidents soon follows, and Liza finds herself in a web of intrigue over the inheritance of the great house. Can she escape alive? Or will the curse of the second house claim yet another victim?

V. J. BANIS

◆

THE SECOND HOUSE

Complete and Unabridged

LINFORD
Leicester

First published in Great Britain

First Linford Edition
published 2015

A catalogue record for this book is available
from the British Library.

ISBN 978–1–4448–2266–3

Published by
F. A. Thorpe (Publishing)
Anstey, Leicestershire

Set by Words & Graphics Ltd.
Anstey, Leicestershire
Printed and bound in Great Britain by
T. J. International Ltd., Padstow, Cornwall

This book is printed on acid-free paper

1

Although it may be a cliché, it is none-theless true that little things often have momentous effects. When I first found Hepzibah she was only a kitten, a poor wet bedraggled thing who could not decide whether she would die from starvation or from drowning. Yet it was this harmless creature who brought Jeffrey and me together and began for me a season of steadily mounting terror that made my life a night-mare. Jeffrey. La Deuxieme, that house with its haunted corridors. Tales of ghostly nuns who wandered the earth to mourn their brutal deaths. I would have known none of these had not a litter of kittens been tied in a bag and thrown into a river to drown.

I nearly drowned myself in that river. When I thought about it afterward, I could almost hear Aunt Gwyneth saying, 'She always acted without thinking. I can't say I'm surprised this happened.'

And it would be true, I suppose, but on this occasion there wasn't time to think.

I had gone for a walk in the country, as I often did. My home was not a happy one and although Aunt Gwyneth warned me over and over that the doctors would send me to the sanitarium again, I spent as much of my time as possible in the out-of-doors, alone. I did not mind so much being alone; it seemed to me that I had been alone all of my life. I was twenty-one now. I had been only four when an accident claimed the lives of my parents, and I scarcely remembered them. I had been six when rheumatic fever claimed me, and since that time I had spent ample time indoors, in hospitals and sanitariums and sickrooms, alone except for the efficient and invariably aloof doctors and nurses who hovered about.

I could not expect Aunt Gwyneth to understand how much it meant to me to go out of her gloomy, unloving house and into the sunshine and fresh air. What did the risk of a chill matter, in exchange for the smell of sweet clover and golden-rod? Her words to me were always practical struggled through water that was waist-high, then chest-high, until I was almost swimming. I could only move with maddening slowness. The bag had drifted downstream, but to my relief it caught on a branch dangling into the water. I prayed that it would hold there until I reached it. Just beyond that point the river grew wider and deeper, and I would never have been able to reach the sack if it were carried into that part. I was barely able to manage where I was.

It seemed an eternity before I reached the sack and could clasp it in my cold hands. I stood for a moment, gasping for breath. I was not very strong physically and I had expended very nearly all of my energy getting to these helpless creatures. Now for the first time I thought of what I was doing, and I was afraid. As out of breath as I was, I did not think I could make it back to the bank. Nor could I remain where I was until I caught my breath. The water here was nearly to my chin and it required all of my strength to resist the swift rush of the water that threatened to sweep me away.

With grim determination I struck out for the bank, but it was no use; I knew almost as soon as I started that I was beaten. My feet slipped out from under me and the water rushed over my head with a cold woosh of sound. I tumbled and splashed helplessly, head over heels. I tried to swim but could not; gasping for air, I swallowed instead the chill green river water. Still clinging to my prize I felt myself being rushed downstream, my lungs violently protesting the watery intrusion. The thought flashed through my mind that I was certain to drown and I could only pray for a miracle.

I got my miracle, if only in the nick of time. Dazed and frightened as I was, I somehow fancied that I was being attacked by some creature of the deep. I didn't know what exactly, I could hardly think clearly, but something brushed against me and then curled about me, and in my fright I struggled against it, trying to free myself.

Suddenly my head was above water. That first gasp of air and the flash of sunlight in my eyes, so shocking after the

6

murky greenness, was like a slap in the face to an hysterical person. I realized at once that what had encircled me was the arm of a man, and that he was trying to save me. He was swimming and tugging me toward the shore.

'Don't fight,' he said. 'I'm not much of a swimmer myself.'

I stopped struggling then and clung weakly to him. In a moment he said breathlessly, 'It's shallow here, try to stand down.' I did so. I had enough sense still to realize that my poor rescuer was only slightly less breathless than I was. Together we managed to stumble the rest of the way through the shallow water, to the grassy bank. I still held the fateful sack in my hands. I let it fall gently into the grass and then I myself fell down. My ears still seemed filled with that ominous roaring that I thought signaled my death. I tried to fill my burning lungs with air.

'Are you all right?' my unknown friend asked after a long moment, putting a hand on my shoulder.

I managed to nod my head weakly. 'Yes, I think so. The kittens . . . ?'

I tried to get up but he restrained me. 'I'll look at them. You try to get your breath back.'

By the time he returned I was able to breathe a little more evenly. He held in his hand the tiniest ball of wet, matted fur. At first I thought it could hardly be alive, but when I touched it I felt the gentlest stirring of its breath.

'The others were already gone,' he said, putting the kitten tenderly into my hands. 'And this poor devil's more dead than alive right now.'

I stared down into a diminutive face and felt a wave of affection sweep over me; the intense pleasurable pain of caring. 'But it is alive,' I said.

'Thanks to you.'

I looked up and for the first time really looked at my companion. He was smiling, and perhaps it was that he had just saved my life in the water, but with the blue sky behind him he looked quite like I had always imagined angels to look. He had what is described in romantic novels as a sensitive face, framed with dark curls. His complexion was tawny, and his wide dark eyes and his deeply colored lips made me think he was Italian.

'And I'm alive, thanks to you,' I said, warming to his smile. 'Where did you come from anyway?'

He nodded toward the road — we had come out on that side of the river — and when I looked I saw a bright red sports car, the door open on the driver's side, informing me that he had left it very much in a hurry.

'I came along just in time to see you jumping into the river with all your clothes on. That didn't suggest to me that you were merely going for a swim. Then I saw you were after that burlap bag, but by that time I had come to the conclusion that you couldn't swim and you were having a bad time of it. So, I came after you as quick as I could. That's all there was to it.'

'I owe you my life.'

My gratitude embarrassed him a little. 'It was beginning to look like all I was going to accomplish was drowning two of us instead of just one. I'm not much of a swimmer, actually, but I am taller than you, so I could keep on the bottom most of the way. Luckily I had to do very little actual swimming.'

'I suppose you must think I'm a very foolish girl to have jumped in like that after a sack of kittens.'

'I think you're a very brave one,' he said, looking at me soberly.

Something happened to him in that moment. I not only sensed it, I could actually see it in his eyes. They seemed to grow darker. I had a sensation that he had suddenly come to a conclusion about something; that the answer to some long worrisome problem had finally occurred to him in that moment that he studied me.

He said, in a lower voice, 'You're very beautiful.'

I was too astonished to think of anything to say, and could only stare dumbly at him.

'Has no one ever told you that before?' He looked surprised by my surprise. I shook my head solemnly. No one had. It was not the sort of thing a doctor was likely to say to his patient or that a nurse would remark upon, and physical beauty was not a matter upon which Aunt Gwyneth put much importance.

'Then you've certainly spent your time with the grandest bunch of dolts in the world.'

I suddenly had a vision of myself as I must look just then — my hair hanging in wet strands about my face, my clothes clinging wetly to me, one shoe lost somewhere in my swim. It struck me as extremely funny that anyone should choose that particular moment of my life to call me beautiful. I couldn't help myself — I began to laugh.

At first he looked at me curiously, but after a moment he realized the joke and began to laugh with me. I held my dear wet kitten to my breast and thought what idiots we must look, wet and bedraggled, sitting in the grass by the river, heads thrown back, laughing ourselves silly.

The laughing spell passed finally, but it had served to dispel the tension lingering from our escapade. We might have been long-time acquaintances; we were so at ease with one another. The kitten stirred in my hands and I held it up to look at it more closely.

'Heavens, you look starved as well as drowned,' I said. 'I think it would be a good idea if I got you home quickly and got some food into you.'

He helped me to my feet. 'I think you'd better let me drive you home. You're already courting pneumonia, without pressing your luck.'

'Yes, I suppose I'd better,' I agreed. Aunt Gwyneth's house wasn't far, but it was on the opposite side of the river, and I didn't think I was up to another crossing.

'I'm Liza Durant,' I said, offering him my free hand.

He smiled and took it warmly. 'Good grief, I forgot we hadn't met. It seemed like we'd known each other forever. I'm Jeffrey Forrest.'

So he had felt it too, that sense of intimacy? In myself I had been willing to shrug it off as the result of not having had friends; that makes one eager to seize upon them when they do appear.

It was surely something more than that, however. I didn't know just what. I felt that my young rescuer had shared many of my own experiences. I had a certainty that he too was very lonely, and very unhappy. I could see from looking at him that he was not an awfully strong person and it occurred to me that perhaps he too had been ill. In any case, we certainly shared a rapport that was astonishing in its spontaneity.

'Forrest,' I repeated as we walked up the bank to the road. 'I rather thought you were Italian.'

'It's the eyes, I got them from my grandmother. She was Italian, a Countess in the old country. But I'm afraid the rest is just ordinary upstate New York.'

I smiled to myself. Upper state New York he might be, but I very much doubted if Jeffrey Forrest could be called ordinary.

Nor was his car. 'Lamborghini,' he said in answer to my question. The name meant nothing to me but the low-slung silhouette and the gleaming wire wheels did. It looked like money.

I gave him directions to Aunt Gwyneth's house. 'You're not a local resident,' I said, more as a statement than a question. I knew most of the people who lived nearby.

'No, I'm in the area on some business.'

'If it brought you along this road, it must have to do with farming. I'm afraid that's about all there is here.' I raised an eyebrow. He did not look like a farmer to me.

He laughed. 'To tell the truth, I suppose someone else should have come in my place; I haven't much of a business head. Today, for instance, I was playing hooky. It was such a beautiful day, and the countryside so inviting, that I was just rambling.'

'It's lucky for the kitten and me that you were,' I said. Then, since he offered no further information, I added, 'If you're going to be here for a few days, and want to play hooky again, perhaps you'll let me show you some of the local sights. There are a few interesting ones.'

'I should like that very much,' he said. I indicated the drive ahead. He turned neatly into it, and we were there.

'I suppose I should invite you in to dry off,' I said.

'I'm afraid it's the clothes that are wet, and I think I'd look a little peculiar borrowing your things.'

We laughed together, and shook hands. 'Take care of the little one,' he said. 'We went to such lengths to salvage her it would be a shame not to.'

'Since it's really you to whom she owes everything, perhaps you should pick a name for her.'

He thought for a moment, and said, 'Let's make it Hepzibah, then.'

'Hepzibah it is.' I held the now dry ball of fur up. Her eyes were open by this time, and she gave me a hesitant meow. 'I think she said she approves.'

'I think she said she's hungry,' he said. 'Tomorrow?'

'Yes, tomorrow would be fine, about one.'

As I watched Mr. Forrest drive away, raising dust from the road, I thought that it was good that we both liked Hawthorne.

★ ★ ★

Aunt Gwyneth was more than a little surprised to see me in my present condition. She listened in silence while I explained; afterward she made up for the silence with a very long narrative concerning primarily my foolishness and the question of how she could be expected to keep a house clean if it was to be filled with cats.

'Not cats,' I corrected her, 'cat. Only one poor little frightened kitten. Hepzibah, meet Aunt Gwyneth.' Not all of Aunt's scolding could lessen my good spirits.

'We'll have hairs everywhere, in the upholstery, in the food — they never stop shedding, that's what I know about cats. You'd better go up and change; I expect it will be back to the hospital for you next week. You'd better take your temperature while you're up there. What did you say that young man's name was?'

'Forrest.'

'I don't remember any Forrests about here.' Had there been any, Aunt Gwyneth would certainly have remembered.

'He's from New York,' I said, starting up the stairs. 'New York state.'

'I suppose we ought to be grateful to

him, of course. Still, it seems to me that you ought to have brought him in for me to meet, him being a stranger and all.'

I had reached the landing. Just as I went around the turn in the stairs, so that she would have no opportunity to reply, I called down to her, 'You'll meet him tomorrow, he's coming to call.'

As soon as I was changed into dry clothes, and determined that my temperature was surprisingly normal, I looked after Hepzibah. My first consideration was food, and I brought some warm milk up from the kitchen. She was so very young that it was necessary to show her how to drink it, but after a few tastes of a milk-dipped finger, she got the idea, and greedily cleaned the dish, purring loudly all the time. In the meantime, I found a box and some old rags, and made up a bed for her. Another box with sand provided for her toilet needs, and she was soon quite at home.

I was in the habit of taking an afternoon nap, and this particular afternoon I felt I needed it more than usual. No sooner had I stretched out over my bed when Hepzibah began crying, and nothing would quiet her but that I bring her up onto the bed with me. Still purring happily, she curled up on the pillow beside me and gave evidence of her own exhaustion. I fell asleep with her happy rumbling in my ear.

The addition of that tiny creature made a vast change in my life. For the first time I knew what it was like to love and be loved. True, it was a far cry from the romantic dream that a young woman ordinarily entertains when she thinks of love, but my life had not been ordinary. Certainly it had been singularly lacking in any sort of affection.

Now, quite suddenly, I had a living thing that idolized me, that followed me everywhere, that rubbed against me and purred for me and licked my face when I held her close. I was not only loved, I was needed. And how I adored this helpless little ball of fluff. We were two creatures who had hitherto been unwanted, had nearly died together, and now lived together. In my heart I was actually grateful to that horrid man who had abandoned that litter, although I grieved too that I had not been able to save them all.

Of course, Hepzibah was not my sole reason for being happy. Jeffrey Forrest came exactly on time that following day. I had to introduce him to Aunt Gwyneth. She was coolly observant. He was shy but quite pleasant. I think I was a little relieved that they did not especially like one another. After a civil time, Jeffrey and I went out. He had asked after Hepzibah immediately upon his arrival, and on departing he suggested we take her along. I was delighted, and she seemed equally so when I made a place for her in an old wicker basket and set her on the seat beside us.

Virtually all of my time outside of hospitals had been spent in the few miles surrounding our home, so that I knew almost every rock and tree by heart. I had said the day before that there were some sights worth seeing, and it was true. We had no skyscrapers nor massive peaks nor breathtaking gorges; ours was only a small farming community, but within an

19

area of a few miles there were the remains of an old Indian fort, and a still-working water mill. In the very heart of town was one of the state's oldest buildings, used for nearly two hundred years as a newspaper office.

'And this,' I said at our last stop, 'has nothing to recommend it except that it's one of the loveliest spots I know.' We had parked by a hill, and mounting this had before us a view of a rambling slope that led downward to a clear fresh stream. Beyond that were green pastures, and in the distance a farm so picturesque as to seem unreal. The lettering on the side of the barn still advised us to chew Mail Pouch.

'You're quite right, it is lovely,' he said, putting down a robe he had brought from the car. We sat on this and Hepzibah was quite delighted to be let out of her basket. She had no difficulty in remembering Mr. Forrest and divided her attention between the two of us as we talked.

'You have a distinct advantage over me,' I said, chewing on a blade of grass I had plucked from the ground. 'You now

20

know virtually everything there is to know about me, my home, my life, and I know nothing about you.'

'Have you never been to upstate New York?'

'No. I've done very little travelling. To and from hospitals, that's about all.'

'It's quite a lovely area. Our home is called La Deuxieme. If you were a history buff, you'd have run across the name in a book or two.'

'La Deuxieme. The second?'

'The second house, in our case.'

I propped myself up on an elbow. An orange and black butterfly hovered nearby as if preparing to listen too. 'It sounds intriguing,' I said. 'Do go on, tell me about this history. Is it romantic?'

'Very,' he said. He seemed happy to speak of his home, and perhaps a little embarrassed by his own pride. I thought as he talked that this story was very old to him; he had heard it first when he was far too young to understand, and a hundred times since then, and when he held a child of his own on his knee, this was the story he would tell him.

'Before the second house,' he said, 'there was, quite naturally, a first house — a convent. A band of French nuns built it before this country was a country. They had set out from the coast thinking they would find a place in the West where they were most needed. Heaven knows how they survived their journey through what was then truly a wilderness. They had no guide with them, not a single man to assist them.

'Somehow, though, they came to a small settlement. The settlers living there were French immigrants who had decided to make their homes in this vast fertile valley bordered with rich forests. There were numerous French settlements in the state. It was still a toss-up, you recall, whether the country would end up French or English.

'The sisters felt at home among this band of countrymen and they felt that they had come to the place where they were needed. Of course it was a long way from what we consider the West, but they had no comprehension of the size of the country, and by their reckoning they had come a very long way. They decided this was where they would stay.'

He paused briefly before going on. 'So, while the settlers built their homes the sisters built their convent. Don't ask how they did it. That's been a mystery all these years. Perhaps they had more help from the townsmen than tradition records. At any rate, for its time and location it was a handsome building. Parts of it still stand. Some of it was wood, and some of it stone, and it was complete with arches and naves and everything one would expect from a prosperous French convent in the old country.

'And the sisters did prosper, as well as the village. It grew quite rapidly. The largest family among the settlers was a silver-smithing family and this became the chief trade for the settlement. These people wrote to relatives and friends at home, who in turn made the difficult journey to the settlement. The convent served as a school for the town, and as a hospital, in addition to being a home for the sisters. And in a short time it just wasn't big enough. Only a few years after the sisters first arrived, they were faced with the necessity of building a second house.

'After some discussion with the towns-folk it was decided that the first building would become a community building; initially it had been outside the town but the town had now crept around it. This time the townsmen took charge of the construction and in a short while the new building was nearly finished. The old building was still referred to as the *couvent*, and the new one simply as La Deuxieme.

'But it was never finished, at least not for the sisters. Tragedy struck. The plague suddenly entered the village. For all the progress, conditions were still primitive. The location was remote. There were neither doctors nor medicine in the village to cope with anything of this sort, and none less than a week's travel away at the very least. The disease spread like wildfire. Entire families were wiped out. The sisters did all they could, but that was all too little. Their convent was filled completely with the dead and the dying;

there were not even enough able-bodied men to keep up with the task of burying the dead. A doctor arrived, summoned by a pair of brave sisters who had risked the wilderness alone to bring him. But he had far underestimated the seriousness of the situation; the medicine he brought was literally a drop in the bucket.

'The rest of the story is quite horrible. You must remember that nearly all these people were simple peasants, volatile and as superstitious as everybody else of that time. By now it was known that the disease arrived with a nun who had just come from the old country. And because the sisters took many of the ailing into their convent it was literally a breeding ground for the plague. Resentment against the place began to grow. People began to say that the sisters were being punished for some wickedness, and the townspeople were suffering as well. One of the villagers in particular, half mad with grief because he had lost his wife and three children, harangued the townspeople, turning them against the sisters. Nearly two hundred people, all but a handful of the town's population, had died within a matter of weeks. Finally, the remaining villagers drew up a sort of petition, asking the sisters to leave in order to lift the curse that had descended upon the village. The sisters refused.

'A short time afterward a handful of men — either with or without the blessings of the rest of the village — set fire to the convent — the original building, that is to say. It was during the night. The timbers were blazing fiercely before the sisters even woke from their slumber. Probably the sisters were meant to escape, but the fire seems to have burned faster than anyone expected. It is not known if any of them escaped alive; if they did so, they fled and never returned. The ruins were filled with the ashes of the sick and the nuns alike.'

He paused for a long moment.

'How horrible,' I said. I shuddered as I envisioned the flames reaching to the sky. I could almost hear the cries of the terrified sisters as they found themselves trapped in the inferno.

Jeffrey too seemed completely absorbed

in his story. For a time he stared thoughtfully before him as though weighing the crime that had been committed.

'Afterward,' he went on, but less somberly, 'the people were ashamed of what they had done. They met and concluded that there were too few of them left, and the town too haunted with tragedy, to make a home there. They gathered together, the few who were not afflicted by the disease, and moved west. As they left, they fired the village, burning it completely to the ground. Only La Deuxieme, still unfinished, was left standing. No one had the heart to set the torch to it.

'A few years later one of my ancestors, in reward for some service to the British throne, was given a vast land grant in this country, including the area of La Deuxieme, which was by then under English domination. My family found the unfinished house and because it was quite a handsome structure, finished it. It's been our family home ever since.'

'What a strange story,' I said when he had finished. 'Those poor creatures, to die so horribly, for no fault of their own.'

'Yes.' He paused. 'It's said they haunt the ruins of the convent, and even wander the halls of La Deuxieme. Tradition is filled with tales of their visits.'

'Are you afraid?' I asked it as a joke, in a teasing tone of voice, trying to restore the lighter mood that had prevailed before, but as I asked, I glanced at Mr. Forrest's face, and I was surprised to see it darken. It was very brief, as though a cloud had passed momentarily between him and the sun, but it gave me a peculiar sensation of foreboding.

'No,' he said, 'not of the sisters.'

The way he said it, however, left me with a curious knowledge; he was not afraid of the ghostly nuns, but he was afraid of something else.

'Good Heavens,' he said suddenly, breaking the somber mood that had settled over us. 'It's nearly three. Your aunt will be after my scalp, or yours.' He jumped up and helped me to my feet. Then he put a squealing Hepzibah back into her basket.

'I'm not at all afraid of my aunt,' I

assured him. 'Or her temper.'

'I have a feeling that you aren't afraid of anything,' he said, folding up the robe we had been seated on.

Again I had that curious knowledge of more than was being said. There was in his voice an envy of my fearlessness. And yet I knew that this man was no coward; certainly he had risked his own life to save mine, hardly the act of a fearful man.

'I don't suppose I am,' I replied aloud.

'Not even death?'

'Least of all death,' I said. I did not add that familiarity breeds contempt, that I had lived so much of my life in the shadow of death, that the specter frightened me not at all.

As we started up the hill I laughed. 'Heavens, aren't we morbid though. Tell me, what brings you here? You said business, I believe.'

'Yes, there's a small silver shop near here. A very fine craftsman has had it for years, and for years we've been trying to induce him to join up with us. The Forrest family is in silver — good and bad, but the money's all been made on plate, at least the last few years.'

'Oh.' I stopped short. 'Silver plate. Of course, how stupid of me. La Deuxieme. The second service, as your ads put it.'

He bowed before me with a gallant wave of his hand. 'At your service.'

We both laughed, and once more we were at ease. But I had been given a glimpse of how much La Deuxieme meant to Jeffrey Forrest; more, surely, than I could fully grasp from that simple glimpse his story had given me. That tale had been more than a traditional legend to him; it had come from deep within him. The sense of horror that the tale created was in part, and in a way that I could not understand, his horror. In time it would become my horror as well, but I did not foresee that on this sunny afternoon as we drove gaily back to Aunt Gwyneth's.

Jeffrey — he insisted on first names before the day was out — came again the next day, and the next after that. I was very happy that he did so. It was the first time I had ever had a close acquaintance. I vaguely felt that I meant more than that to Jeffrey; and in a sense, he meant more to me as well. In the first flush of our meeting, I had wondered if this were to be my grand amour, my knight in shining armor.

I quickly realized that I was not in love with Jeffrey, at least not in the sense that I understood romantic love, but I did love him, with an affection that was nearly shocking for having been so quickly established. I felt closer to him than to anyone else I had ever known. I felt so close in fact that, although I knew we would never be lovers in that true sense of the word, I did not stop myself from wondering what a future with Jeffrey would be like.

I knew that he was handsome, sensitive, more inclined toward the arts than toward business. Enjoying his visit, but producing no success in his business mission, he had nevertheless sent off telegrams to his father that gave every reasonable excuse for staying on. I knew too that Jeffrey was wealthy and would be vastly more so at the death of his father. I had a notion that he was somewhat spoiled; he himself said that he was essentially a coward and lazy.

'But you risked your neck to save me,' I protested.

'An impulse,' he said. 'It was so romantic, the lovely young woman drowning to save a sackful of kittens, I couldn't help flinging myself into it. I don't mind telling you now that when we were fighting that current I was sorry I hadn't let you float downstream.'

I didn't believe him at all. I told him of my illness, and he was surprised. 'Yet you went right into the river after those kittens, knowing you had been sick?'

'Impulse,' I told him. He grinned and grabbed me impulsively, hugging me. That was the first time we had ever embraced. We both knew when it stopped being a silly gesture and became something quite a bit different. It was I who ended it finally, freeing myself gently but firmly from his arms.

We said nothing about it, but when I saw into his eyes, I had a shock. I had never seen it before, and except for the books I had read, I was quite ignorant of the subject, but I was suddenly aware that Jeffrey Forrest was in love with me.

I still did not love him, not in the romantic sense. I had to be honest with myself about that, but I had lived my entire life alone and unhappy. Now, for the first time, I was happy. I had someone whose companionship I enjoyed, someone I liked and with whom I could share simple pleasures, and laughter, and interesting conversation.

I found myself wondering if Jeffrey would propose. In my fancy, I thought ahead to what that life might be like — the wife of Jeffrey, handsome, kind, witty, living in a luxurious mansion haunted with legends of the past. I compared that vision to what my life was and had been. And it would be lonelier still when once Jeffrey went away. Having shared a little of my life with someone, it would be worse still to go back to being alone.

I think he meant to ask me that day to marry him; and I would have accepted. As it happened, though, the moment was shattered for us — shot away, as it were.

We were by the river, at a spot that was

a mutual favorite of ours. Hepzibah, out of her basket, was engrossed in the pursuit of a grasshopper. I was leaning against the trunk of a large elm tree. Jeffrey had been lying beside me but he had gotten to his knees to embrace me.

That embrace had just ended, and we were still close, still gazing uncertainly into one another's eyes. So absorbed was I that at first I did not realize the significance of the loud cracking sound I heard, or the ping of something striking the tree trunk in the short space between our faces.

There was a second crack, and this time a piece of bark jumped from the tree, striking Jeffrey's cheek. Suddenly I realized that the reports were gunshots, and that the bullets had struck the tree within inches of us.

'Get down,' I cried, throwing myself to the ground. Jeffrey fell too, covering me with his body. For a long moment there was silence.

'Some stupid hunter,' I said breathlessly, shaking with anger. We were at the edge of the woods, and hunting, even out of season, was not very unusual.

'Hello!' Jeffrey called. 'Watch out for us.'

There was no answer. After another long moment we got shakily to our feet. 'I wish I had gotten a look at him,' I said, staring in the direction from which the shots seemed to have come. 'He'd hear about this before I was finished.'

Jeffrey managed a faint laugh but when I looked at him I was quite shocked. He was far more shaken than I. He had gone absolutely white.

He said, 'It's lucky for him you didn't, I guess.' He got Hepzibah and put her into her basket. Taking my arm, he started me quickly along toward the road. 'Come on, I suppose we had better get away before he spies another rabbit or whatever he was after.'

In the car, and on the way home, we both tried to make jokes about the incident. For all his attempts at humor, however, I could see that Jeffrey remained very upset by what had happened.

He scarcely took time to say goodbye before driving away from Aunt Gwyneth's house.

2

I suppose that I should have known then that danger hovered about Jeffrey Forrest. I had imagined myself Jeffrey's wife; I had seen myself living in luxury, in comfort — and in happiness. But the omens were all there for me to see, and my failure to see them must have been a deliberate form of blindness on my part.

At first I had attributed that shooting to some careless hunter, but later as I reflected upon it, this seemed less and less reasonable. I had been dressed in red and blue, hardly inconspicuous colors, and Jeffrey had been wearing a yellow shirt. Only a nearly blind hunter could have failed to see us.

If not an accident, though, what? Surely not a deliberate attempt on our lives. I had no enemies locally; having spent so much of my time in hospitals, I hardly knew anyone well enough to have earned enmity.

As for Jeffrey, how could he have

enemies when he knew no one at all here? He had come to the area on a business mission, true. He was here to attempt to persuade a local silversmith to join his company, but surely that gentleman, whose name he had told me was Lescott, would have no motive to try to shoot Jeffrey. If the business offer were not to his taste, he could simply say 'no.' I doubted that Jeffrey was particularly stubborn in his persuasion.

No, there was no one about who had any motive to shoot at either of us, and I was left with the awkward, but obviously correct, theory of an accident.

I was mistaken in thinking, however, that there was no one in the area who knew Jeffrey. The very evening after the shooting I had occasion to meet another member of his family.

Jeffrey and I had taken to having dinners together several nights a week. Sometimes we ate at Aunt Gwyneth's house, where I prepared dinner for all three of us. In my years of convalescence I had learned to cook well, and I enjoyed the task.

Other times Jeffrey and I ate out, so

that we could be alone. We were not, on these occasions, particularly romantic with one another, and very little of our conversation could not have been made in Aunt Gwyneth's company. The simple truth was that Aunt Gwyneth and Jeffrey were not awfully fond of one another. So, one or two nights each week, I joined Jeffrey in the dining room of the little hotel at which he was staying; it was the only really nice restaurant in the town. The food was well prepared, if not particularly exotic, and the atmosphere was quiet and intimate.

We had arranged to have dinner at the hotel that particular night. I saw, as soon as I arrived, that Jeffrey was still quite upset over the shooting incident. Although it was on my mind too, I deliberately tried to put a good face on things, to cheer him up. By the time our desserts — freshly baked apple pie — had arrived, he seemed relaxed and happy again. His moods changed swiftly, as if curtains lifted and fell to hide or reveal the dark brooding landscapes of his personality.

He was telling me a funny little story of

an incident in his childhood. We were so engrossed in our conversation and laughter that I did not even see the man who approached our table. I was suddenly aware that someone was standing there, looking down upon us. We looked up; I heard Jeffrey gasp.

'Guy,' he said, scrambling to his feet.

For a moment I could do nothing but stare at this handsome creature who had descended upon us. He had a certain resemblance to Jeffrey, except that he was taller and more powerfully built. The features that on Jeffrey's face were delicate and sensitive-looking were, on this newcomer's countenance, ruggedly handsome. He wore a frank expression that made you certain you would know at any given moment just what he was thinking and how he felt toward you.

I became aware, as he looked from Jeffrey to me, that he did not feel kindly toward me, although I could imagine no reason why this should be so.

I had been so busy gawking that I had almost been oblivious to the introductions Jeffrey was making. Dimly I heard him say, 'Miss Liza Durant, may I introduce my cousin, Guy Delane.'

I put my hand in his. He looked so swaggeringly nineteenth-century I nearly expected him to bow from the waist and kiss it, but he only shook it gently and released it. He was not overly enthusiastic.

'I thought Jeffrey had no relatives in the area,' I said.

'Guy is from New York,' Jeffrey said. 'And this visit is a surprise. What brings you here? I hope the family isn't so dissatisfied with the results I've produced that they thought you'd be needed?'

'From what I've seen, there haven't been any results,' Guy said. It was an insulting remark, and Jeffrey's frown showed that he resented it. He did not reply though.

'Of course, it's not hard to see how you've been diverted,' Guy added, with a glance in my direction.

'I hope I haven't caused any difficulties,' I said, smiling, although I disliked this sort of rudeness. 'I find it difficult to imagine myself diverting men from their legitimate pursuits.'

'He's quite right,' Jeffrey said. 'If ever a lady was born to turn men's heads, it is you.' He put a hand upon my shoulder. I knew that he meant it to reassure me in the face of Guy's rudeness, and perhaps he meant also to take strength from me. Strangely, though, I found myself unaccountably resenting this gesture. It seemed intimate, and possessive. I saw too that Guy noticed it at once. He smiled in a mocking manner. His manner, barely short of leering, angered me. I reached up and put my hand over Jeffrey's.

'You two have become well acquainted, it seems,' Guy said.

'Miss Durant is a good friend,' Jeffrey said.

'You've known one another such a short time.'

'It is very easy to like your cousin,' I said. 'He inspires one's trust and affection.'

Mr. Delane gave me the benefit of another of his mocking glances. 'The men of our family are quite accustomed to meeting young ladies who, upon learning of our position, find us easy to like.'

My face burned crimson. Even Jeffrey, who was obviously accustomed to being intimidated by the more aggressive personality of his cousin, flushed angrily. 'That is uncalled for,' he said sharply.

Guy's smile only flashed more brightly. 'Then I apologize, of course. In any event,' he said to Jeffrey, 'I did not come here because of your lack of success in dealing with Lescott. I came because your father is ill. Gravely ill, in fact.'

Jeffrey grew pale at this news. For a moment he had nothing to say, and when he spoke it was to say simply, 'I see.'

I had no emotional involvement with this news, of course, except that I felt sympathy for Jeffrey. This being the case, I could view things with somewhat more detachment. As a result, I found myself wondering why Guy Delane had come such a long distance to deliver this news in person. There were telephones here, and I thought Western Union still delivered messages. Had the two been more obviously fond of one another I might have thought it an act of kindness; but I didn't think it was affection for Jeffrey that had prompted Guy to make the trip.

Why, then, had he?

I reminded myself that I knew nothing, after all, of the intra-family relationships of this clan. Perhaps this was merely the way they did things, personal animosity notwithstanding. And, lest I forget, it was really none of my business.

'I've made arrangements for us to return tomorrow,' Guy went on. 'I assume that is satisfactory?'

'Yes,' Jeffrey said. 'In that case, I have some business I want to take care of this evening. With Mr. Lescott, as a matter of fact. You see, I haven't been entirely without results, notwithstanding my distractions.' He gave me a nod.

'Then you've interested Lescott in joining Forrest Silver?' Guy asked.

'I think so. He was to let me know in the morning, but it can't harm anything to see him this evening. He may have made up his mind already.'

'Shall I join you?'

Jeffrey gave his cousin a cold look. 'I don't think that will be necessary,' he said.

'I am the firm's general manager,' Guy said, apparently unperturbed by Jeffrey's coolness.

'And my father is still the principal owner,' Jeffrey replied. 'And I am here at his instructions to carry out a specific task. If you will pardon me, I will finish it myself.'

Guy shrugged and said, 'As you wish.'

Jeffrey turned to me. 'You'll come with me, won't you?' he asked.

'If you like,' I said, standing. I thought it actually pointless, since I could do nothing to help him in his business efforts; but I felt that inviting me was an act of defiance directed toward Mr. Delane, and being none too happy with that gentleman's manner, I was only too glad to go along with Jeffrey's wishes.

I gave Mr. Delane my hand again. 'It's been most pleasant,' I said.

'A singular experience,' he murmured.

As we left I felt Mr. Delane's eyes upon me; they were not, I was certain, approving.

I dismissed the incident from my mind. I will probably never see him again, I told myself.

I was wrong.

3

Mr. Lescott was in the little shop that he kept. Although it was closed, he opened it for us when he recognized Jeffrey, locking the doors after us when we had come in.

'This is Miss Durant,' Jeffrey introduced me. 'She's been very graciously entertaining me while I've been in your town.'

'How very fortunate for you,' Mr. Lescott said. He bobbed his head in my direction. He was a small man, wizened and drawn, but with no suggestion of frailty. He seemed to have taken on some of the gleam of the precious metal with which he worked. His face shone, and his eyes were bright.

'I've admired your work,' I said. 'There are so few real artisans left.'

He nodded his head. 'Yes, it's true, it's true. And we are sinking beneath the river of factory production.'

'There are factories, and factories,'

Jeffrey said. 'You've seen the work we do at our place. We try to maintain high standards. We put out a great deal of hand-wrought work, some of the finest. If you came with us, you could have a completely free hand to do the kind of work you want to do, the way you want to do it. The difference is that your market would become worldwide instead of just here.'

'Yes,' Mr. Lescott agreed. 'I have thought of all this. Frankly, I am barely making a living here. I work for the joy of working, of course, but a man must eat.'

'Then you'll come to New York?'

'I'll come,' Mr. Lescott said. At Jeffrey's happy smile, he raised a warning hand. 'Only to have a look,' he said quickly. 'And to see what it might be like. If it's as you say, then — we'll see. Is that agreeable?'

'Yes, certainly,' Jeffrey said. He looked delighted and I could not help smiling with him. I knew without being told that his delight in part was the satisfaction of telling Guy Delane he had brought the agreement off.

They made their arrangements. Mr. Lescott would not be able to leave quite so quickly as Jeffrey, but he would plan on coming to New York in about a week. The arrangements would be made for his travel. A room would be rented for him near the factory so that he could work at whatever hours best suited him.

It seemed completely satisfactory to everyone concerned. We bade Mr. Lescott good night, and left him to his lovely pieces of silver. Jeffrey and I walked back to his hotel.

'Thank you for coming with me,' he said, taking my hand in his affectionately. 'I think it helped convince him.'

'You're welcome, of course,' I said, 'although frankly I can't imagine how my presence helped.'

'A pretty face is always an asset,' he said. Then, more soberly, he said, 'I'm sorry my cousin was so rude.'

'It's nothing, really,' I assured him. 'I haven't led so sheltered a life that I've never met a rude man before.'

'It may make more sense to you if I explain something,' he said. 'Here, let's sit for a moment.' A wooden bench stood by the sidewalk, for no reason other than to offer passers-by a resting place. He took my arm and steered me over to it, bidding me sit down.

'Guy Delane does not live at La Deuxieme,' Jeffrey said. 'That is a fact he bitterly resents.'

'I somehow assumed that he did live there,' I said.

'He wishes that he did instead of me. Over the years there have been countless claims to the property — some of them quite laughable, some of them not so funny. They've involved not only out-siders, but family as well, and they have been the cause of more than a few bitter quarrels.

'Guy lives with his mother at Hamlyn Hall, a smaller place nearby. His grand-mother and my grandfather were sister and brother. The Delanes have always claimed a right to the estate, but traditionally the Forrest estates have passed from first born to first born, and Guy's grandmother had to be content with Hamlyn Hall — it was, then, part of the same properties, and my grandfather needn't even have given her that.'

I thought to myself that his generosity did not sound great to me, but I did not consider it my place to become involved in their family quarrels. To a family as old as his, traditions no doubt weighed more than any other consideration.

'They receive monies from the factories, which Guy runs. And if I should pass on without a wife or heir, Guy would inherit controlling interests in the Forrest estates. La Deuxieme would in effect be his then.'

'But of course you will be marrying someday,' I said. 'You will have heirs. So poor Guy will have to be content with what he has.'

I laughed as I said it, but somehow it did not seem likely that Guy would be content with what he had. He was the sort of man to see things that he wanted and to reach out and take them. I wondered that he had not managed somehow to take La Deuxieme from Jeffrey's not-too-powerful grasp.

The answer, of course, was that Jeffrey

was not yet the master of La Deuxieme, not so long as his father lived. 'I hope,' I said aloud, 'that your father will get better.'

He sighed and shook his head. 'So do I, but it isn't likely. He's been going downhill badly. He's nearing seventy.'

'That's not so awfully old,' I said.

'It is when you've lived as dissolute a life as he has,' he answered. He gave my hand a pat. 'But I've spent enough time boring you with the Forrests and their problems. Come on, I'll take you home.'

He was silent as he drove me to Aunt Gwyneth's and I made no attempt to start up a conversation. I was thinking how much more lonely I would be when he was gone; I supposed he was thinking something similar.

When we arrived at the house I invited him in, but he declined. 'Guy will be banging on my door early and I like to have my wits about me when he's around,' he said.

He took me in his arms and kissed me, gently at first and then with more ardor. 'Liza, you do care for me, don't you?' he asked when the kiss was ended.

'Yes,' I said, without elaborating. I think he knew that my affections for him stopped short of being in love; in any event, he did not push the matter that far.

He kissed me again. 'I'll be in touch as soon as I can,' he said.

We said goodbye, and he left.

I did not try to see him off the next day. I thought he would have other things on his mind than me, and anyway, I did not particularly want to see Guy Delane again. I could not imagine why he disturbed me so much as he did. I found that whenever I tried to think of Jeffrey, Guy intruded upon my thoughts, smirking, mocking me.

I did not expect to hear from Jeffrey right away — indeed, I had resigned myself to the possibility that I might not hear from him at all. I had had no experience with such things, but I knew of shipboard romances and the like. I knew that away from home, in a strange locale, a man may take a fancy to a woman who, when he has gone home and thinks about her, will prove after all to be of no great interest to him.

Had I been truly in love with Jeffrey, that possibility might have frightened me more than it did. But I was not, and while it saddened me, it left me with no great burden of grief. I liked Jeffrey, I had enjoyed our time together, and certainly it would give me pleasure to see him again, but in my life to date happy times had always been brief, and one becomes inured even to a sense of loss.

I fell into the pattern of living that had been mine before he came. I spent my time alone, or rather, in the company of Hepzibah, who sometimes seemed to be questioning me about Jeffrey's absence. I walked and wandered and read. I revisited some of the places we had visited, and found myself wishing Jeffrey were with me.

Two days after Jeffrey had gone, I was surprised to see the car belonging to our postmaster pull up outside the house. I went to meet him at the door. He was bringing a special delivery letter for me.

It was from Jeffrey. It said simply that his father had died, and that he would be in touch with me very soon.

I sent off a quick note of my own expressing my sadness at Jeffrey's loss. I wondered what sort of man it was who had died — a man, I felt certain, of strong will. I sensed that Jeffrey had been frightened of him (although I felt Guy Delane probably had not been). As I did not know him, however, I could only conjecture as to what his death would mean to Jeffrey in particular, and to the Forrest family in general.

I knew from our conversation that Jeffrey was the chief heir to the estate. He was the first born, and it was tradition in the Forrest family that the first born inherit. My knowledge of the estate was limited, but I knew that there was much property involved, and of course the silver works, which was a large and varied operation. I envisioned entire armies of attorneys, heirs, friends and the like descending on Jeffrey in the days following his father's death, and I resigned myself to the fact that I would not see or hear from him in weeks.

I was doubly surprised, then, when he telephoned less than a week later. We received few calls at Aunt Gwyneth's, certainly rare few long-distance calls. Dear Aunt Gwyneth was positively atwitter when she came into the parlor to tell me that there was a New York call for me.

'Darling,' Jeffrey greeted me. 'I've missed you something awful.'

'I've missed you too,' I said. It was the first he'd ever used that affectionate term for me; I could not know, of course, that it was for the benefit of other ears than mine. 'How are things going?'

'Just rotten, if you want to know the truth,' he said with a chuckle. 'I feel as if I've been penned up with a herd of dragons — is that the right word for dragons, herd?'

'I'm sure I don't know,' I replied, laughing. I was flattered that Jeffrey should be calling me, especially at what must indeed be a hectic time for him. And, I admit it, a little puzzled, too.

'I'm coming to see you,' he said out of the blue.

'Are you really? When?'

'Right away.'

It was so unexpected that for a moment

I could think of nothing to say. 'Do you think you should?' I asked after a moment. 'I mean, you must have a thousand things to do there. And one does have to be practical.' I would never have told him so, but I was envisioning Guy Delane's disapproval. I knew what he would have to say about Jeffrey's running off to see me at a crucial time like this — although why his approval or disapproval should matter an iota to me I couldn't say.

'I have something much more important to take care of,' Jeffrey said. 'And I am being practical. I'll be there the day after tomorrow, all right?'

'Yes, certainly it's all right,' I said. 'I mean, I'm not going anywhere. But I still don't think . . . '

'Thursday, then,' he interrupted me. 'I love you.'

There was a silence. I suppose he was waiting for me to say the same. But I was so dumbfounded at his having said it that it never occurred to me to reply.

After a moment, he said goodbye, and rang off.

Not until I was seated in the parlor did

the import of what he had said come clear. The 'darling', the 'I love you,' the statement that he had to come to see me right away, that he had important things to take care of. Perhaps I was reading too much between the lines, but I suddenly thought that I knew why Jeffrey was coming. I thought that he meant to propose to me, ask me to become his wife.

What, I asked myself, would I answer?

Did I want to be Jeffrey Forrest's wife? My impulse was to say yes. It seemed to signify an end to the loneliness I had known all of my life. I was fond of Jeffrey, and he was more than fond of me. He was handsome, witty, sensitive, charming and kind. He offered wealth of the sort most young women only dream of. I knew that he would do everything in his power to make me happy.

But was my happiness within his power?

There was another consideration as well. Jeffrey had just lost his father. However much he did or did not love that man, the loss would be a shock. There was not only the family tie to consider. Jeffrey had just inherited a vast fortune and vast responsibilities as well. I do not think he took well to that sort of burden. It would not be hard to suspect that Jeffrey's thinking was a little less than clear just now.

I knew too that he looked upon me as strong and courageous, and I wondered if he were not simply trying to tie himself to my apron strings as it were, to borrow my strength. In accepting his proposal, I might be taking advantage of his present confusion, and borrowing future unhappiness for both of us.

It crossed my mind too that Guy Delane would certainly snicker when he heard of the plans. I could well imagine what he would have to say about my marrying Jeffrey.

In the end, however, I came face to face with one certain fact — I hadn't been asked yet. I was stewing about bridges that my road might never bring me to. For all I knew, Jeffrey was coming on some sort of business errand — not Lescott, however, because that gentleman had already closed up his shop and left for New York. That I had investigated at once.

Jeffrey arrived on Thursday as expected. He phoned to say that he was at the hotel and would like to have dinner with me. As luck would have it, my social calendar was empty for the evening, and I accepted.

Moreover, I took great pains with making up and dressing. Quite by coincidence I had seen a new dress in a shop window the day before and, because it was exactly my color, I had bought it. I wore that, a fluffy pale yellow affair, and a yellow rose in my dark hair. Hepzibah meowed her approval at me. I picked her up and held her to my cheek, enjoying the rumble of her purring against my skin.

'Tell me, little one,' I asked her, meeting the limpid gaze of her eyes, 'what does the evening have in store for me?'

Her answer was a yawn. I hoped she was not predicting how the evening would be.

Jeffrey was waiting, looking impatient. He was obviously delighted to see me and in truth I was rather happy to see him. It had been lonely in the days since he had departed, more so than I had realized until he was back.

'It's good to be with you again,' he said when we were seated at our table, and our wine had been poured.

'I was just thinking the same,' I said. He leaned closer to take my hand.

'I've come to suggest that we don't need to be apart in the future,' he said. 'I realized when I left how much I loved you. We haven't known each other a long time, that's true, but I think there's been a rapport between us since that first day. I felt then that you would be important to my future.'

He paused, watching me closely for some reaction. I smiled and said, 'Yes, there was something that clicked then, wasn't there?'

'I'm not doing this very well,' he said, laughing a little under his breath.

'Probably no one does,' I said.

'I want you to marry me,' he said.

4

I knew that it was cruel to sit in silence, not answering him, but for a moment or two I had no answer to give. Although I had considered this possibility, perhaps had even hoped that this was why Jeffrey wanted to see me, I still had come to no conclusions

'Why do you want to marry me?' I asked finally.

He seemed confused by the question. 'Because — because I love you, of course,' he said.

'And no other reason?'

'Yes, certainly, if you want practical motives,' he said. 'I'm master of La Deuxieme now. I'm expected to marry and produce heirs. And I'm lonely there, too, if that's important.'

And frightened of something, I thought, but I did not say it aloud.

'You know that I'm not in love with you,' I did say aloud. 'Very fond of you, yes, but not in love.'

'I think that's enough. I think I can make you happy. You'll be mistress of a fine old house. We get on well together. And there's really nothing to keep you here, is there?'

'No, you're right there,' I admitted. After a pause, I said, 'Let's make a deal. I have no real conception of what you are offering me so far as a home or a way of life. I don't know that I would even like it at La Deuxieme. And neither of us knows whether La Deuxieme would like me.'

'It doesn't matter whether they do or not,' he said impatiently. 'I'm the master there now.'

From the passion of his remark I knew that I would not be welcomed by the others in the family. It was not hard to understand why, of course. With Jeffrey unmarried, the others of the family were in line to inherit. If he married, their inheritances would go to his heirs instead. No, there would be no open arms welcoming me there.

And I did mean to go.

'It matters to me,' I said. 'In any event,

I think it would be precipitous to marry so soon after your father's death.' He started to object, but I silenced him with a look. 'I *will* come to La Deuxieme, however, to sort of get the lay of the land. It will be a good opportunity for us to see one another under different circumstances from what we've had here. Who knows, I may really fall in love when I see you surrounded with the family wealth and luxury. They say silk sheets make a hedonist of every woman.'

I smiled to show that I was only joking, and of course he took it in kind. I could see that he was not entirely pleased with my offer, but he seemed resigned to going along with it. He already knew how stubborn I could be when once I had made up my mind to something.

'Once I've gotten you there,' he said, 'I may not let you leave.'

Neither of us knew then how prophetic those words were.

Because his business was so pressing, it was decided that Jeffrey would return without me, and that I would join him in a week, when I had had time to shop for some clothes I felt I needed — my present wardrobe had not been purchased with an eye to house guesting with a moneyed family — and take care of other details.

Aunt Gwyneth was among the 'other details'. It was true she had no particular claim on me, nor I on her, but we had been together a while, and she had assumed the responsibility, however unwelcome, for my welfare. Not surprisingly, she disapproved of my plans for traveling to New York.

'In my day,' she said, sniffing, 'a young lady did not go traipsing off on a trip of that sort unescorted.'

'It's not as if I'm being invited to Mr. Forrest's bachelor apartment in the big city,' I pointed out. 'His whole family is in residence there, as I understand it, from aunts right on through. He assures me we'll be chaperoned day and night. And anyway, I won't be alone. Hepzibah will be with me.'

Hepzibah seemed pleased with that announcement; Aunt Gwyneth was somewhat less enthusiastic.

'Of course you'll do as you please,' she said coolly. 'I've never stood in your way.'

'Oh, Aunt, dear, I know,' I cried, seeing that she was more wounded than I had expected. I put my arms about her. We rarely displayed that sort of affection toward one another, and she was a bit nonplussed. 'And I love you for it. But this may be the one grand experience of my life. Surely I'm entitled to one wild, romantic adventure?'

She recovered her poise after a minute. 'Yes,' she said, giving my shoulder a pat. 'Yes, I suppose you are.' She drew back and looked at me searchingly. 'I've done all that I could do, but I'm not such a fool that I don't know it has never been enough.'

'It's been a great deal,' I said. It was true, she had done so very much, and she was no more to blame than I if our love for one another was a minimal thing. The coincidence of family ties is not enough to make two people care very much.

'You'd be a complete fool,' she said, not reproaching me or herself, but simply stating facts, 'if you were content with nothing more from life than what I can give you here. Yes, go to this strange-sounding place. It may be nothing more than a wild goose chase; it may produce nothing but disappointment and sadness; it may simply produce nothing. But you're a clever girl, and strong-minded. I have no doubt you'll look after yourself.'

She freed herself from my embrace and turned away before she added, 'Of course, you can always come back here if it doesn't work out right.'

I found her offer deeply touching. It is one of the perversities of human nature that we care most for another's company when we foresee that we are losing it, through death, parting, or whatever. I felt closer to Aunt Gwyneth than I had before.

It was a big step. I was going several hundred miles. I faced a new lifestyle, strangers, unknown places and things.

On the other hand, I had so little life to give up, that it was not so difficult for me as it must be for others. I had no job to retire from, no house to close up, nothing to go into storage. There were a few things that I would not be taking — books, records, and the like — but I merely left them in the bedroom that was mine, and closed it up. If it should turn out that I would not be returning they could be shipped along later.

I had some shopping to do, mostly to buy new clothes. I had luggage, which I had packed for God alone remembered how many trips to clinics and sanatoriums. But the suitcases and clothes that were suitable for that purpose were not what I wanted to take on this trip. Aunt Gwyneth, to my surprise, helped me with the preparations. I do not think I do her an unkindness to say that, beneath her concern for me and a certain sense of loss, she was probably looking forward to having me away for a while. She was a woman who enjoyed her freedom as well as I enjoyed mine and inevitably I must have at times been a nuisance.

A week after Jeffrey's proposal of marriage, I left to join him.

* * *

How can I describe La Deuxieme? It was splendid of course, and somewhat smaller than I had anticipated. I had expected something in the French style, because of its name and its legend of French nuns. I was surprised to see a house in the English manor style.

'But the area was predominantly English by the time this house was built,' Jeffrey answered that question for me. 'The nuns had little more than the shell built when the tragedy occurred. My family finished it in the English style that they admired.'

One came upon the place suddenly, as it were. It was set in a little valley so that you did not see it as you came down the narrow road. The road mounted a little hill and there was the house before you. It was beautiful and awe-inspiring and at the same time it gave you a sense of sadness, perhaps because one knew of its legacy of death and heartbreak. We drove down the long lane, headed by splendid gates, past rows of tall trees that I could not identify. The lane broadened into a graveled parking court, and there we were. I sat for a moment in the car staring at the house which might be my home someday. I shivered, as if someone had just walked across my grave.

'Frightened?' Jeffrey asked, helping me from the car.

'Why should I be?' I asked, but I was only evading his question. I was frightened, and I hardly knew why. Of course it was all new to me, and I had almost nothing with me to give me a sense of familiarity. If only I had brought Hepzibah; I had wanted to, but Aunt Gwyneth had pointed out, wisely, that it would be presumptuous as a house guest to show up with a pet. For all I knew the Forrests might loathe cats. In the end I had come without her, but already I missed her affectionate presence.

In part too it was that Jeffrey was frightened; nor was this some vague impression on my part. He was nervous and ill-at-ease, and had been since meeting me at the station. I thought he had something that he wanted to tell me and he had not yet brought himself to confessing; but if such were the case he had kept it to himself during the drive up to the house. He seemed to anticipate some sort of unpleasantness, and his anxiety was contagious. I approached the house with dread instead of the pleasurable excitement I had expected to feel.

We were scarcely inside the house, just in the hall, when we were joined by a tall, handsome woman whom I should have recognized at once as Jeffrey's sister, even had I not known he had one. She might almost have been his twin, they looked so much alike. I knew from Jeffrey's descriptions of his family that she was widowed.

'Hello,' she greeted me, 'I'm Ellen Forrest, Jeffrey's sister. Welcome to La Deuxieme.'

She was not unfriendly in her manner, although I detected an air of curiosity and perhaps, although I might have been imagining this, the faintest whiff of resentment. Her manner seemed intended to remind me that she was the hostess here and I only a guest.

'How do you do?' I greeted her. 'I'm very happy to be here.'

A young man had followed her into the

hall. He was less attractive than she was, or Jeffrey. He lacked the slim elegance of the Forrests, but was stocky and somehow clumsy-looking. He had a petulant expression as he bluntly looked me over.

'This is my son, Paul,' Ellen said, introducing me to the young man.

'How do you do?' I greeted both of them. 'I hope my coming hasn't inconvenienced you.'

'Not at all. It's always a delight to have Jeffrey's friends here.' She stretched up to kiss her brother's cheek. I wondered if her remark meant to put me in a place as merely another of Jeffrey's friends. Just in case, I put my arm through his and leaned against him a bit possessively.

In this word game, however, it was Jeffrey who scored the coup. 'I'm afraid I've kept something from you, Ellen,' he said, giving my arm a squeeze. 'Liza isn't just a friend.'

I smiled inwardly, but my smile froze as he continued: 'She is my wife.'

How I managed to retain any poise in the moments that followed his announcement I shall never know. I kept saying to myself, over and over, *you've kept that news from me, too.* I think the smile remained plastered on my face. Luckily I have the habit of keeping shock to myself, hidden behind a bland exterior.

Ellen was indeed surprised, and not happily so, I thought, but she recovered more quickly than I, and put an arm about me to hug me. 'I wish you every happiness,' she said.

I replied with some inane remark, I don't recall what. Young Paul said something too, and then Jeffery was piloting me up the stairs, whispering in my ear, 'I'll explain in a minute,' and insisting to the others that I was tired from the trip and wanted to rest.

'Have you lost your senses?' I demanded as soon as we were in what presumably was my room, with the door closed after us. 'Why would you tell them . . . ?'

He warned me with a finger to his lips. 'Not so loud,' he said. He took my arm and led me across the room. Two chairs and a little Victorian table were positioned by a large window so that they enjoyed a view of the hills and a not-too-distant wood. I sat, and he pulled the other chair closer and sat facing me. I was not so much angry as bewildered, but I saw, when I met Jeffrey's eyes, that he was deeply troubled over something. I swallowed the stream of questions I was about to ask, and forced myself to be patient.

'I wanted to talk to you on the way up here,' he said, smiling wanly. 'I should have; I'm sorry to have sprung that on you so suddenly down there.'

'It was a bit of a surprise,' I said, managing to return his smile. It put him a little more at ease, but only for a moment. His anxiety returned as quickly as it had gone. He stood and began to pace up and down before the window.

'I should have explained before then,' he said. 'Before you came here. I'm such a coward.'

'I don't think you a coward,' I said quietly. He was working himself into some sort of state. I had never seen him so agitated. A frightening thought crept into my consciousness. I knew very little about Jeffrey. I knew about his family, his home, the silver business, even the ghostly nuns from the past. The truth was, however, I knew very little about the man before me.

I turned that thought aside and drove it from my mind. It was disloyal and unkind. I knew that he had saved my life and that in the time since he had been a good friend to me, always courteous, thoughtful, gentle. Surely I owed him a few moments of patience, at the very least.

'I brought you here because I am afraid,' he said, turning back to me. His face certainly echoed his words. He looked not only frightened but nearly hysterical, and I felt that whatever he was trying to explain to me he had been holding in only through an effort of will.

'I think my father was murdered,' he said.

It was so sudden, so unexpected, that it was a moment before I felt the shock waves emanating out from that statement. All of a sudden a chill swept over me.

'What makes you say that?'

'This,' he said. From his pocket he produced a medicine bottle. I had seen enough of those in my time. I took it from him and read the label; it contained insulin, and it was nearly empty.

'It's insulin,' I said. 'Was your father taking it?'

'He was. Or at least, he was supposed to be. That's the thing. That isn't insulin in that bottle. It's nothing but plain water.'

I looked up, startled. 'Then you think — you think someone withheld his medicine, to hasten his death?'

'It raises the question, doesn't it?'

'Then you ought to call in the police,' I said, handing the bottle back to him. He put it in his pocket again.

'It doesn't prove anything,' he said. 'There's no evidence that he really was given injections from this vial.'

'Where did you come by that?' I asked.

'It had been thrown into the trash. All the medicine had, which made me suspicious, particularly when no one admitted to having disposed of it. I dug it all out and looked it over carefully.'

I thought for a moment. 'I'm afraid it's pretty slim,' I said. 'After all, from what you've told me, you're the one to benefit from his death. Don't you inherit?'

'Have you forgotten, someone shot at us a few weeks ago?' he asked.

'But that was an accident, surely,' I said. I did not really believe that myself, though.

'Was it?' he asked.

I had no answer. I could only look back at him in silence.

'I told you before,' he said, 'La Deuxieme has been plagued with claims, fights over the rightful ownership. In my desk there's an entire file of letters, lawsuits, affidavits, and the like. There's been much bitterness in the past, even violence. It's the legacy of those nuns. This place was born in tragedy, and it will die that way.'

He spoke with such fervor that I was frightened anew and instinctively drew back from him.

'If you think your father was murdered,' I said, 'and that someone wants to kill you as well, why did you bring me here? And how does all this fit in with telling your family that we are husband and wife?'

'You're my protection,' he said. I must have looked quite dumbfounded. 'Don't you see,' he hurried on, 'my father is dead; I am the heir to La Deuxieme. But if I died, unmarried, without an heir, the estate would be up for grabs, in a manner of speaking. Someone with a strong enough will and enough determination to have La Deuxieme for his own could wrest it from the grasp of the others and become master here.'

'But if you're married,' I said, beginning to understand.

'I have an heir,' he finished for me. 'There's no point now in killing me. As my wife, you would inherit, not they.'

I was so stunned by this revelation that I could think of nothing to say. Jeffrey looked so triumphant; he quite obviously felt that he had cleverly managed to forestall his own doom.

All this was sheer madness. I could not conceive of the sort of intrigue of which he spoke; medicines withheld, people shooting at other people in the woods, disputed estates . . .

That was it, of course. I had never been

close to the sort of wealth and power and importance that La Deuxieme represented. I could little know what people might do for it.

Another thought occurred to me. Perhaps, literally, it was madness. Jeffrey was not a particularly strong person, nor a particularly stable one. I had known that from the first. His father's death and the great responsibility that death had thrust upon him had without doubt been a great shock to him. Could all this be the workings of an unsettled mind and a vivid imagination? I had thought earlier that Jeffrey looked nearly hysterical; how sound was his reasoning just now?

'I hardly know what to say,' I said, standing also. 'Or do.'

He seized me by the shoulders. His grip was strong, so fierce that it seemed to braise the flesh. 'Then do nothing,' he said, pleading with me. 'Go along with my charade, at least for a few days.'

'Until?' I asked, raising an eyebrow.

'Until I've had time to sort some of this out in my mind,' he said. It was as if he too knew that his thinking was not entirely clear. 'This is our suite of rooms,' he said. 'That door leads to a sitting room, and beyond it is another bedroom. I'll use that one, so you needn't fear any sort of impropriety.'

When I still hesitated, he added, passionately, 'Please.'

I sighed. 'I will stay, and I will go along with the pretense of being your bride . . . ' His face broke into a smile, but I added quickly, ' . . . for tonight only.'

'And tomorrow?' he asked.

'We'll see,' I said. I did not want to commit myself fully to the sort of deception he wanted of me. It was not only a matter of ethics; I was simply not confident that I could bring it off for any length of time. I needed a night to think it all over before I decided.

'I guess that's fair enough,' he said. 'I'm grateful, really, Liza.' He took my hand in a more gentle manner. 'And anyway, it isn't such a big lie. I really want you to be my bride, in case you've forgotten.'

'I haven't forgotten,' I replied. 'That is why I came, after all.' I did not add that it apparently was not why he had asked me.

78

'I'll have Marie bring your things up,' he said, reverting to the role of charming host. 'Dinner is at eight. I'll be in the other room, if there's anything you want or need.'

At the door he paused to say, 'I want your visit here to be as pleasant as possible.'

But it had not gotten off to a very pleasant beginning, I thought as he went out. How could I be comfortable here, under the circumstances? On one hand was the possibility that Jeffrey was right, and that a murderer watched us and waited for an opportunity to make some further move. On the other hand, Jeffrey might be unbalanced by the things that had happened of late.

Neither of these possibilities struck me as particularly pleasant. Despite the fact that I was genuinely fond of Jeffrey, and despite the fact that La Deuxieme was as lovely a place as I had ever seen, I was beginning to regret that I had come. Aunt Gwyneth, with her uneventful life and uninspired cottage, seemed suddenly more desirable.

I went to the window and looked out across the hills. It was a lovely view, and had a tranquilizing effect on one. How foolish the schemes of men seemed when one saw the beauty and order of nature.

I had not told Jeffrey the one thought that had troubled me since he had told me his fears. If someone wanted him dead, for the sake of gaining control of La Deuxieme, and if that someone had been responsible for the shooting incident that had occurred to us — then that someone could only be Guy Delane. He was the only member of the family who had been in that area at the time.

Another thought entered my mind as well. If someone wanted the estate badly enough to kill Jeffrey, surely they would not hesitate to kill his heir as well.

And, as his alleged bride, I was that heir.

5

I came down to the dining room promptly at eight, making every effort to look poised and calm. I did not feel either. I had had enough jitters over meeting Jeffrey's family without the additional unpleasantness of Jeffrey's fears. Fortunately no one set upon me with daggers, or pounced upon me from a dark shadow, and after a few minutes I began to relax and to soak up impressions of my dinner companions.

During the afternoon Jeffrey had told me a little about the others living in the house, so that I would not be completely in the dark. In addition to his sister Ellen, who was widowed, and Paul her son, there were an Aunt Lydia and a cousin, Walter.

Jeffrey was fond of his aunt. She had raised him after his mother's early death, and his attitude toward her was more that of a son than a nephew.

'But you may as well be forewarned,' he said. 'She's no longer entirely in possession of her faculties.'

'You don't mean she's mad?' I asked. I hoped I had not brought myself into a house filled with mad people.

He laughed and shook his head. 'No, although I think sometimes she tries to give that impression. She's just a little senile. Sometimes she gets confused about things, or starts imagining things.'

If he found a parallel between that and his own behavior, he did not express it, and I kept my thoughts to myself.

As for Walter, he was, in Jeffrey's words, bland. Jeffrey neglected to tell me that Walter had something of a drinking problem. I observed that for myself during that first dinner with the Forrests. I suspected that Walter had been drinking before he came down to dinner, and with dinner he put away an inordinate quantity of wine. He was not drunk, in the sense of falling about or being incoherent; but he was not altogether sober either. He slurred his words, and his eyes had a feverish brightness to them.

I was aware that I was inevitably an item of some curiosity to all of them. They had certainly learned by now that Jeffrey was 'married'. They would have been better than most if they had not resented me a little, but for the most part they treated me with courtesy and an apparently sincere effort to make me feel welcome. They were, after all, a well-bred family with whom hospitality was a tradition.

'Our home was begun as a haven, understand,' Ellen said during dinner. 'I suppose Jeffrey told you the legend of our home.'

'Yes,' I said. 'Rather a grim tale, isn't it?'

'The Forrests prefer the word 'romantic',' Walter said, smiling a little lopsidedly at me.

'The Forrests,' Aunt Lydia said from her place at Jeffrey's right, 'are plagued with nonsense. I agree with Jeffrey's young lady. It's a grim story. I see nothing romantic about a lot of nuns being burned alive.'

'That's a little strong for the dinner table, isn't it?' Paul asked.

'I didn't bring it up,' Aunt Lydia

snapped. She swept the assemblage with a cold look that defied them to argue the point with her. No one did, and she returned her attention to the pheasant on her plate.

I was rather taken by the old woman. She seemed quite in possession of her faculties this evening. She was blunt and commanding, but she had wit and charm, and she was genuinely warm toward me.

'I'm glad to see Jeffrey's found someone pretty and with some character as well,' she said out of the blue, nodding in my direction. I had been given the place at the foot of the table. Jeffrey, as master of the house, sat at the head. It had never occurred to me that, as his wife, I would have the place of the mistress; but I could hardly refuse it without making a scene, and revealing the truth, that Jeffrey and I were not yet married. I had somehow expected a place well below the salt. All in all, and Jeffrey's fears notwithstanding, I would hardly have blamed them if they had poisoned me that first night, for usurping their places.

'I can't imagine what makes you say

that on such short notice,' I said, as everyone looked in my direction.

'I can tell,' she said. 'I've been around a year or two, my dear. I can spot a ninny a mile away. Most of the Forrests are ninnies.'

'Aunt,' Ellen objected.

'Ninnies,' she said. 'And fools.'

'Which am I, do you think?' Jeffrey asked in a teasing manner, less perturbed by her remarks than the others at the table.

'I would have said a fool until I met her,' she said. 'But I've had to revise my estimate of your intelligence.'

'What a stroke of luck for me,' he said, winking at me down the considerable length of the table.

'I know better than to ask her opinion of me,' Walter said. He emptied his glass — I had lost count of the times he had already done so — and promptly refilled it with the decanter before him. He spilled a little on the cloth as he did so. No one seemed to mind, or even to notice.

'For such fools,' Paul said, 'the family's done well. The business is booming.' He looked in my direction. 'Has Jeffrey informed you that you're marrying a great deal of money?'

'I assumed he was not poor,' I said coolly.

'The business is booming,' Aunt Lydia said, ignoring any innuendos directed at me, 'because my brother, Jeffrey's father, managed it very well, and because since then Guy has managed it, also very well.'

'Guy will rob us blind someday,' Paul snapped. 'He'd like to see all of us dead and buried.'

'Which proves how sound his judgment is,' the old lady replied.

I felt a chill run down my spine at this turn in the conversation. It was too akin to what Jeffrey felt, and the thoughts I had entertained since my conversation with him. Dead and buried! Those words echoed through my mind. I did not look at Jeffrey, but I knew he had reacted to that remark too, and I felt that he was watching me.

'I must apologize,' Ellen said to me. 'Our family seems to spend all too much time in bickering.'

'I don't think that's awfully unusual,' I said. 'When I've gotten the drift of it, I'll probably be putting my two cents' worth in.'

I was glad, though, when dinner was over and I could bid the others good evening and retire to my own rooms. It was a warm evening, and I had left the windows open. A spring breeze wafted through the bedchamber, making the curtains billow. I could not help thinking how lovely the place was, and how much I would probably enjoy it if I were here under some other circumstances.

Soon after I had gone up, I realized that I had left my handkerchief in the dining room. It was a lovely lace one, a gift from Aunt Gwyneth, and I did not want to lose it. I left my room and made my way downstairs again. I did not see anyone stirring about. I did not know how the occupants of the house filled their hours, but presumably they had their own interests.

The dining room was across the hall and slightly nearer than the library. The doors of both rooms were open, and as I came near I recognized the voices of Jeffrey and Ellen in conversation in the library. I did not go in, but retrieved my handkerchief from the dining room and started back to my bedroom.

I did not mean to eavesdrop on the conversation in the library, but I could not help overhearing a scrap of it.

' . . . You married that girl under false pretenses, and you know it,' Ellen was saying. She sounded angry, as if they were arguing, and this prompted her no doubt to raise her voice slightly, so that I heard her plainly, while Jeffrey's reply was lost to me.

'It's true,' Ellen insisted. 'Does she know about the hospital? Does she know it's been only a few months since you were discharged from a mental institution?'

I gasped, putting a hand to my throat. A mental institution? No, Jeffrey had said nothing of that to me. Yet, from the very moment I heard it said, I knew that it was true. His instability, his moods, his inability to stand up to life — yes, he was the sort who would suffer a 'breakdown' at a time of crisis.

Their voices had dropped again. I went on, hurrying up the stairs, not wanting to spy on them.

In my room again, I went to the window and looked out at the night.

Was Jeffrey mad? He was going through another time of crisis right now; had it unsettled his mind? Were his fears nothing but the result of fantasy, a fiction that he had spun for — for what reason?

Before I had been vaguely afraid; part of it had been inherited from Jeffrey, fear being as contagious as any disease, and perhaps more deadly. Now suddenly my fear was real and my own, and it was not La Deuxieme or the ghosts of nuns, or some faceless enemy that frightened me. Although it shamed me to admit it even to myself, I was afraid of Jeffrey.

I had locked the door from the hall into my room. I went to the connecting door that led to the sitting room, and through that to Jeffrey's room, and locked that door as well.

In the morning, in the light of day, Jeffrey would have to answer some questions before I decided to remain here and continue this charade.

This was what I thought as I prepared for bed. I had no way of knowing what the night held, or that Jeffrey would never answer the questions that I was forming in my mind.

How could I have foreseen that by morning he would be unable to answer my questions?

★   ★   ★

I knew almost before I woke that something was wrong. The entire house had an air of activity, of alarm. Tragedy seemed to hover in the air.

My room was still dark with the lingering shadows of night when, shortly after dawn, I was awakened by a knocking at my door. I started to tell whoever it was (Jeffrey?) to come in; then I remembered that I had locked the door when I came in the night before. I struggled into my robe as I crossed the room to answer it.

It was the housekeeper; I thought I remembered that her name was Marie, but I was still too burdened with sleep to be certain. I had met her the previous night. She was dark and grim-faced. I assumed that she was efficient, or had been with the family for years. Certainly friendliness and charm were not her strong points.

She looked even more dour this morning. 'Miss Ellen asks you to come downstairs at once,' she said, without a prior greeting. 'There's been a bad accident.'

'I'll be right down,' I said. I saw her glance beyond me. I realized too late that Jeffrey and I were supposedly married, and that he ought to have been in bed with me. I pushed the door partially closed, but I knew she had already seen he was not there.

'My husband is in the bathroom,' I said, knowing that it sounded false. 'I'll tell him.'

I did not know until later how foolish that explanation was. She gave me a startled look, and nodded. When she was gone, I hurried through the connecting sitting room to the door of Jeffrey's room, and knocked. There was no reply.

'Jeffrey,' I said in a low voice, opening the unlocked door — he, presumably, had anticipated no danger from me. But there was still no answer, and when I looked in I saw that the room was empty. His bed, unmade, was empty. I could only guess that he was already downstairs; which explained why the housekeeper had looked so startled when I had said that he was in the bathroom. I would have to cover that slip when I came down, I told myself.

I did not know the cause of the summons, or how major the alarm was. I thought it discreet to take a moment to slip into a dress. It was quicker to pull my hair back and tie it with a scarf than to take time to comb it out. Only a few minutes after I had awakened, I was on my way downstairs.

The housekeeper had not said where I would find the others, but my guess of the dining room proved correct. Ellen, Paul and Walter were all three there. The housekeeper was just bringing in coffee from the kitchen when I came in. They all turned toward me.

It was Ellen who spoke. She looked

haggard and strained; of course, it was very early. 'What time did Jeffrey get up?' she asked.

'Why, I don't know,' I replied, surprised by the question. Then, remembering that I was supposed to have shared his bed, I added, 'I'm a very sound sleeper. He must have gotten up and gone out without waking me.'

Suddenly I realized that, except for Aunt Lydia, Jeffrey was the only member of the household not in the room. 'Why?' I asked. 'What's happened?'

'There's been an accident,' Ellen said.

I had a presentiment of what she was going to say. A chill went through me.

'Jeffrey is dead,' she said.

The room seemed to sway. Walter — he was sober this morning, and seemed much more in command of himself — came quickly to me, putting an arm about me.

'Easy,' he said. 'Here, better sit down.' He led me to a chair and helped me into it.

I was so stunned that my wits all but deserted me. 'What happened?' I asked in a voice that was little more than a hoarse whisper.

'He's been drowned, in the lake,' Walter explained in a gentle voice. 'The gardener found him in the water just a short while ago.'

'The lake?' I looked up at them, unable to comprehend what I was hearing. I knew that there was a small lake nearby, beyond the ruins of the old convent, although I had not yet seen either of these spots. But it was only just after dawn; Jeffrey must have drowned before dawn. I could not imagine what he had been doing there at such an hour.

'What was he doing at the lake?' I asked aloud.

Ellen shook her head. 'We have no idea. We were just asking ourselves the same question when you came in. I had hoped perhaps you'd offer us some explanation.'

I shook my head dazedly. 'I can't imagine,' I said.

'He may have been going for a swim,' Paul suggested.

'He told me he didn't swim very well,' I said. 'But even assuming that he was out for that reason, was he in the habit of swimming before dawn?' I asked. It was possible, of course, that he did just that. I knew little enough of his personal habits.

'When he was younger, sometimes,' Ellen said. 'But not in several years. And you're right, he wasn't much of a swimmer. He mostly just splashed about.'

'He's fully clothed,' Walter said. 'Hardly the way one would go swimming.'

'Then he went for a stroll,' Paul said.

'Before the sun had even come up?' Walter seemed doubtful.

'If he had trouble sleeping . . . ?' Paul offered, and gave me a questioning glance.

'I don't know,' I said. 'As I told you before, I sleep very soundly.' That was true, so far as it went. I could not explain that he had also slept two rooms away from me and that even if I had been a light sleeper I would not have been likely to hear him rise and leave his room.

'We've sent for the authorities,' Ellen said. 'You might as well have some coffee. I'm sure they'll want to talk to all of us.'

Walter brought me a cup of steaming coffee. 'Thank you,' I said, taking it gratefully. We did not try to keep up a conversation. Each of us seemed to have his or her own thoughts to dwell upon.

Only a day before, I was thinking, Jeffrey had voiced his fears to me, fears of death. And now he was dead, drowned in a manner that seemed puzzling at the least. Had he been murdered, as he had feared?

He had spoken too of the tragic legacy of La Deuxieme, a legacy of death and grief. He had inherited that along with this estate. He was one now with the ghosts that haunted this place.

6

The local sheriff came a short time later. He was a kindly-looking man whom I would have taken probably for a doctor, or even a priest, rather than a man of the law. I thought of the sort of crimes he must ordinarily investigate — family quarrels, some youthful pranks at Halloween, perhaps a tourist driving too fast. And now he was confronted with death, and a mysterious death to boot.

'I know how unpleasant this is for everybody,' he said, when we were assembled in the dining room. 'For you especially, Mrs. Forrest,' he said to me, 'coming here only yesterday a bride, and today finding yourself a widow.'

I thought, now is the time when I must state the truth, correct the false impression they have.

I did not, without fully understanding my reasons for not doing so. I did not understand Jeffrey's death. I knew that he had feared that he would die, and my pose as his wife had been a desperate effort on his part to save his life. There were too many things I wanted to know, too many questions in my mind. I smiled my gratitude to the sheriff for his sympathy, and kept my silence.

'Is everyone here?' he asked, looking about.

'Aunt Lydia's in her room,' Ellen said. 'It's been a blow to her. I don't think she would be much help.'

The sheriff seemed to understand the implication of the remark; Lydia had presumably slipped into her senile state at the news of Jeffrey's death.

'I didn't call the help in,' Walter said.

'That's all right, I'll talk to them later.'

The housekeeper, whose name was indeed Marie, came in just then. 'May I speak to you a minute?' she asked Ellen.

'Surely,' Ellen said. She excused herself to us, and followed the gaunt woman into the kitchen.

She returned in a moment, her eyes falling on me at once. 'I think there's something that ought to be brought up,' she said to the room in general. 'Marie informs me that you and your husband did not share the same room last night. Is that correct?'

'Yes,' I stammered, blushing. I seized upon the first thought that came into mind. 'We had a quarrel.'

The sheriff seemed to find this information most interesting. 'That sort of confirms what I've been thinking,' he said. 'Can anyone tell me if Mr. Forrest had been particularly unhappy — despondent, even?'

'Very,' Ellen answered the question. 'You may as well be told, if you don't already know. Jeffrey has not been well. Some months ago he had a breakdown. He spent some time at a private hospital — a mental hospital.'

'Any particular reason?' the sheriff wanted to know.

'Jeffrey was always unstable, emotional, often even hysterical. He didn't want to go into the business at all. He cared for art, for poetry, for music. Our father pressured him into assuming business responsibilities. He tried, but the pressure became too much for him.'

After a pause, the sheriff asked, 'Do you think he had been straightened out after this, ummm — breakdown?'

Ellen sighed and gave her shoulders a shrug. 'We thought so. He did go back to work. He took a trip for Father recently, a business trip.' She gave me a glance. 'But since Father's death, he's not been well. He's been very upset, and plainly the responsibility has been more than he wanted to bear.'

There was a lengthy silence. I saw where all this was leading and I wanted to say that they were wrong, but I could not deny what Ellen was saying. I had seen for myself that Jeffrey was upset, beside himself, not thinking rationally. I had no doubt that her story of the breakdown and the hospital were true. I had nothing with which to refute her implications.

'A quarrel, coming at a time like this . . .' Paul said, letting the sentence drift off.

They all looked at me again.

'I don't think my husband committed suicide,' I said bluntly, bringing the word into the conversation directly for the first time.

'I'll admit,' the sheriff said, 'it seems strange that a man would do so right after marrying.'

'Forgive me for being frank,' Ellen said, moistening her lips with the tip of her tongue, 'but I can't help wondering if that mightn't have been the subject of their quarrel. I did not get the impression that Miss Durant — ' she caught my raised eyebrows, and corrected herself: ' . . . Jeffrey's bride was — how shall I say it? — a woman in love.'

I felt my face turn red. 'Then why do you think I married him?' I asked, knowing exactly what she was hinting at.

'There may have been other, rather obvious, motives,' she said. 'I'm sorry, my dear, but it has to be said. If my brother, on top of everything else, learned during a quarrel that his wife did not truly love him, that she had married him perhaps for his money . . . Don't you see, it might very well have driven him to the brink.'

'That's rather hypothetical, isn't it?' I asked.

'Did you love him?' she asked in turn. Her gaze was penetrating; it seemed to look right through me.

'Yes,' I lied, but the word fell false even on my own ears. I looked around, and saw on their faces that it sounded no more convincing to them.

I turned to the sheriff. 'Do you believe Jeffrey killed himself?' I asked.

He looked embarrassed at having to reply. 'I don't see what else it could be,' he said, avoiding my gaze. 'He didn't go swimming fully dressed. And all the things I've heard here certainly point in that direction, wouldn't you agree?'

'Might he not have been drowned?' I asked frankly.

He looked at me then, a slightly incredulous expression on his face. 'You mean — murder?'

The word was like the crash of thunder, striking us all silent. That was precisely what I had meant, but the full weight of the charge was awesome.

'Yes,' I said in a smaller voice. 'Murder.'

He shook his head, poking out his cheek with his tongue. 'I can't think why that would even come into it,' he said. 'Why would anyone want to murder him?

Any big fights lately?'

There was a general shaking of heads, and some murmured 'No's.

'There's the house and the family money,' I said.

'But the family's already living here,' the sheriff argued. 'Looks to me like they're living pretty well, too. Why would they want to kill one of their own relatives to get hold of something they've already got?'

I saw suddenly that I could never make him understand what Jeffrey had made me see through his eyes: what La Deuxieme meant to these people. Not just living in it, or having the money to spend, but being master of the place, having it as one's own. That was something entirely different from being allowed here as a part of the family. La Deuxieme and its mastery were something beyond this man's grasp. My efforts to explain to him would be futile.

My shoulders drooped. The sheriff seemed to accept my defeat as meaning I saw I was mistaken. 'No,' he repeated, satisfied that he had convinced me, 'doesn't seem to be a single reason to think of murder, and every reason under the sun to think of suicide. That looks like the only other possibility to me — of course, it might have been an accident. He might have run into the water after something and gotten his feet tangled up in the weeds on the bottom. He is tangled up in them. That might have been it.'

'I wonder if we couldn't settle on that?' Ellen said, speaking persuasively. 'If it is a real possibility, of course. It would be so much less ugly.'

'I'll want to go back out and have another look at the place,' the sheriff said, scratching his earlobe. 'But I don't see any reason why it can't be reported that way.'

It was clear that no one believed it was that sort of accident. They were all convinced that Jeffrey had killed himself.

No, I reminded myself, not all of them. Someone knew better: the one who had killed him.

★   ★   ★

The sheriff went, plainly satisfied with his investigation of the incident and a report of accidental drowning. I kept my thoughts to myself. I was certain that Jeffrey had not committed suicide. It was true he had felt keenly the burden of responsibility that had been put upon his shoulders; but while he had seemed afraid, he had not seemed despondent. Anyway, I knew what the family did not: that he and I had had no quarrel.

Had I done the right thing by keeping the secret of our marital hoax from the family and the sheriff? I had reacted partly in anger at the suggestion that I had married Jeffrey for his money, and partly from a sense of loyalty to Jeffrey. But if I told the truth it would put a different light on the theory of suicide.

Or was I only letting my imagination run away with me, as I had accused Jeffrey of doing? He had been in a mental hospital previously. He had been in a state of mental and emotional strain since his father's death. I myself had wondered if he were thinking rationally. I had even — I was ashamed to admit this now that he had gone — locked my door against him the night before so that he could not come into my room.

And in locking that door, I had failed him. I had accepted within my own mind that he was mistaken, that his story was purely fantasy. Now he was dead.

I owed it to him, and to my own conscience, to remain at La Deuxieme and to continue to pose as his wife, at least until the questions in my own mind were answered. It might well be that he had killed himself; but I wanted to be convinced of that before I left here. And if something else more horrible had happened, I wanted to know.

Jeffrey had pointed out his aunt's room the day before. It was only down the hall from my own. Notwithstanding what Ellen had said about the old lady's mental state today, I wanted to see her. I knew that she and Jeffrey had been fond of one another, more so than they showed to others, and I was certain she was carrying a heavy burden of grief.

I knocked at her door and, at her invitation, came into her room. I found her in her bedclothes, sitting up in bed. She had a book in her hands; I saw, when I came closer, that it was a Bible. No doubt she was seeking consolation from its pages.

'I came to see how you are,' I said, pausing a respectful distance from her bed.

She made a gesture of resignation. 'When one is my age,' she said, 'one accepts these losses more easily. I have been thinking how sad this has been for you.'

A thought flashed through my mind. I had expected to find Aunt Lydia barely coherent; but far from that, she seemed quite in control of her senses and very much aware of what had happened.

'You know about Jeffrey, then?' I asked, aware that I was gambling on an impression. If she did not, if I were mistaken, I could be inviting problems.

'Yes, of course,' she said. 'Come closer.'

Despite her years she had a commanding manner, so that one was inclined to do as she said. I came nearer the bed. She reached out and took my hand in hers.

'I must say things to you that may

shock and alarm you,' she said, looking me steadily in the eye. 'But I must say them now, while my mind is clear.' She saw a protest forming on my lips, and silenced it. 'No, it will do no good to flatter me and pretend that what is, is not. I sometimes get confused over things. It doesn't matter; I little influence the course of events, so I can do no one harm.'

She paused for a moment, as if her thoughts had drifted far away; I was afraid that they had. How quickly did her mind go when it went? I wondered.

'But,' she said abruptly, looking back at me again, 'I want to alter the course of events now, through you.'

'Through me?' I asked, startled.

'There's no one else I would trust enough to say these things to. And we share a secret, you and I.'

She had a crafty look. I had no way of knowing to what she referred. I thought, perhaps, she was not so coherent today.

'A secret?' I asked.

'Regarding your marriage.'

I blushed, and tried to think what to say. Was she fishing? Or did she actually know? 'I don't understand,' I said.

'I think you do.' She winked in a conspiratorial fashion. 'Come, come, didn't Jeffrey tell you he often shared his secrets with me? And his fears. He came to me after his father's death, and told me what he found, and what he feared. It was I who pointed out that he needed an heir. And when he told me you had hesitated to marry him, it was I who suggested that the family need not know that.'

I was astonished. At the same time, it was quite obvious she did know the entire truth, and that there was no point in attempting to deny it.

'Then you knew we were not married,' I said.

'Of course. Don't confuse me with the rest of the Forrests. They're all fools, but I'm not. I'm only crazy.'

I smiled at that. I did indeed like this aged creature. 'I don't think you're crazy,' I said.

'Careful,' she warned me, 'or I may conclude you're a fool too.'

I felt a bond of friendship pass between us. The others of the family had been polite, even hospitable to me, but Aunt Lydia was the only one to act as if I were truly welcome here, as if we might grow to care for one another.

She grew serious again. 'And it is because we share this knowledge that we share another idea as well. Neither of us can believe that Jeffrey killed himself this morning.'

I gasped. It was a shock, hearing my own fears voiced aloud by someone who shared them. 'I don't know,' I said, uncertainly. 'I thought not, but the others . . . '

'Pshaw. He was certain he was going to be murdered. He was in love with you; he wanted to marry you. He had everything to look forward to. Now he is dead. It is imbecilic to think it was a suicide. If a man wanted to kill himself, what a foolish way to do it. It would not be Jeffrey's way. If he were going to do that, he'd have done it quickly, painlessly.'

'It may have been an accident,' I said uncertainly.

'If one could explain in any sensible manner why he was out wading before dawn in a lake that he knew was infested with weeds, and dangerous. No, I don't accept that idea either.'

'Then you believe someone killed him?'

She fixed those piercing eyes on me. 'I do. And we must discover the truth, you and I.'

'But how?'

'You must remain here, at La Deuxieme. You must let them continue to believe that you are his widow. Then you can be my eyes and ears.'

I could not help feeling that I was moving deeper and deeper into a shadowy realm that held danger and heartbreak for me. 'Is there no one in the family who can be trusted?' I asked. If only I had an ally of some sort in the house, someone other than this fragile woman before me.

'Trust none of them,' she said emphatically.

A thought came to me. 'What of the Delanes?' I asked, feeling a tremor of excitement even as I said the name. 'Guy, and his mother.'

She let go of my hand and sank back against the pillows. She looked suddenly very tired. The excitement had been too much for her. I thought for a moment that she might not even have heard my question.

'They're the hardest of the lot,' she said after a long pause. 'Ah, Margaret Delane. There's a woman for you. Hard as nails, and as clever as a fox. We loathe one another.' She paused, smiling, and added, 'But it's a nice healthy loathing. When I was stronger, and ran this house for Jeffrey's father, she was the only one of the entire clan with enough backbone to stand up to me; she and her son. They had gumption, that pair.

'That's what's kept the Forrests in money these last few years, with business everywhere falling off. Guy runs the silver works like the Caesars of Rome.'

My heart lightened at what she was saying. 'Then you think I could trust them?'

She laughed softly. 'You'd be crazy if you did,' she said. 'They'd do anything to get La Deuxieme for their own, including chopping you and me both up with an axe.' She laughed again, while my heart sank.

'Then there's no one . . . ' I began after a moment's reflection, but she interrupted me.

'I tell you,' she said in a rising voice, a childish look coming over her face, 'I tell you I will marry him, and no one can stop me.'

I was completely taken aback. She had changed in an instant. One moment she had been sensible, strong-willed, determined. The next she looked and acted as if she were mad.

I stepped back, and when I did, I lifted my eyes. I saw Ellen's reflection in the mirror over the dresser. I had not heard her come in, but she stood just inside the door, staring coldly at us.

7

'Why are you in here?' Ellen demanded, coming into the room as I whirled about. 'Didn't I tell you that the old woman had had a shock, that she wasn't making any sense?'

'I . . . I was concerned about her,' I stammered, my thoughts whirling through my head. 'I wanted to see if she was feeling any better.'

She went past me, to the bed.

'I will marry him,' Aunt Lydia said loudly, shaking her finger at Ellen's nose.

'Now she's all worked up,' Ellen said. To her aunt she said, 'Very well, dear, of course you may marry him. He's a fine young man.'

'You'll see,' Aunt Lydia went on in her childish voice. 'You won't be able to stop me.'

I backed from the room, watching in frightened fascination as Ellen consoled the older woman in her agitation. In the hall, I turned and nearly ran to my room.

My heart was pounding. How much of our conversation had Ellen heard before Aunt Lydia slipped into senility? And had that one really slipped into senility, or had she seen Ellen before I did, and put on an act to throw her off the track?

There was another possibility as well, one I did not particularly like to face. Had Aunt Lydia really been as sane as I thought, or had all of her conversation been the workings of an unbalanced mind? Perhaps I had only thought it clear because it fell in so neatly with my own fears. And my fears had come, in part, from Jeffrey's remarks. But Jeffrey was unstable too.

I looked at myself in the mirror. My eyes looked large and frightened.

But I couldn't leave. Even before my conversation with Aunt Lydia, I had made up my mind to learn the truth before I went.

If, I thought, sitting on the edge of my bed, they allowed me to stay.

That was only an example of my naiveté. I did not realize that, or my true position here, until later that day when the housekeeper Marie came to my room. I was reading, deliberately keeping to myself until I felt calmer and more confident in my role of widow. Marie was even more unfriendly than before; I supposed she felt a little guilt over having divulged her discovery that Jeffrey and I had not spent the night together.

'There's a Mister Lescott downstairs,' she said to me in a surly tone. 'He wants to know if you can see him today.'

Although I was surprised by the visit, I said, 'Yes, surely, I'll be down in a moment.'

She started from the room; but it occurred to me that I desperately needed an ally in this house. Of all the house's occupants, the housekeeper was the only one with no motive for resenting or suspecting me. It could matter but little to her who of the family was in control, so long as she was retained in service. It would be foolish of me to allow her to continue to be unhappy with me.

'Marie,' I said. She paused at the door and waited for me to go on. 'I'm afraid all these dreadful goings-on have made rather a bad start to my stay here.'

She said nothing.

'I had hoped it could be more pleasant. I had meant to ask you if you couldn't help me — explain some of the routine, tell me a little about the family, that sort of thing.'

'I ain't one to gossip about the family,' she said, curtly. 'If there's anything you want to know about how the house is run, I'll try to answer it for you.'

Chastened, I said lamely, 'Thank you. I'll call on you if I have any questions.'

'Very good,' she said, and went out.

I waited a moment until my cheeks had paled again. Then, checking the mirror to be sure that I looked neat, I went downstairs to meet Mr. Lescott. I had not seen the little silversmith since coming to La Deuxieme, although I knew that he was here. He looked, I thought, younger and healthier than when I had met him back home. The Forrest silver works seemed to be agreeing with him.

'Mr. Lescott, how nice to see you again,' I greeted him. It was true, actually.

Although I felt no affection for him, he was someone from home, a face that I did not in fact associate with La Deuxieme.

'I was sorry to hear of your bereavement,' he said, bobbing his head courteously. 'Such a young, healthy man, to go in such an awful way.'

'It was a great shock,' I said. I paused, and then asked, 'What can I do for you?'

'There's a question I wanted to get clear in my mind regarding my association with the silverworks. It's about my signature on the pieces I do. I know this is a sad time for you, but it's a matter I would like to have clear in my mind as soon as possible.'

I frankly had little idea what he was talking about, and less why he should bring the question to me. 'I don't think I understand . . . ' I began; then, suddenly, I did understand.

I was mistress of La Deuxieme!

Not only Jeffrey's widow, but his heir; mistress of all this vast estate; of this house, of the silverworks. Mistress of the fortunes of the entire family.

I must have looked alarmed, because

Mr. Lescott took a step toward me, his hand out, and asked, 'Are you all right?'

'Yes, yes,' I said. I put out my own hand and steadied myself on the back of a chair. The enormity of my guilt all but overwhelmed me.

I shook my head, trying to clear my thoughts. 'Mr. Delane is still in charge of that business,' I said, composing myself as best I could.

Mr. Lescott looked hesitant. 'I spoke to him,' he said, sounding apologetic for having to pursue the matter further. 'But he said he did not know what your plans would be.'

'I see,' I said. 'I'm sorry to have inconvenienced you in this manner. My — my husband was quite eager to enlist you as a part of our enterprises, and I naturally want to see that accomplished as well, for his sake. If you'll only bear with me . . . I shall see Mr. Delane today and clarify his position. And if you will take your problem up with him, I'm sure he will deal with it to everyone's satisfaction.'

He seemed satisfied with that. 'Of

course, of course,' he said, bowing to me again. He left, again expressing his sorrow.

When he had gone, I sank into the chair before me. What a fool I had been. I was no more qualified to run an estate of this size than Jeffrey had been — much less so, in fact. However ill-suited he might have been to it, he had been raised with it; he knew the business, the people involved, the machinations of handling money. Nothing in my life had prepared me for the role I was expected to play.

There was another realization that sent my heart pounding. If Jeffrey had been right in his fears, if Aunt Lydia was right in her suspicions, Jeffrey had been murdered so that someone could control La Deuxieme.

But in order to gain that control, to reach that goal, the same person would have to deal now with me. I, as mistress of La Deuxieme, now stood in the way.

If Jeffrey had been murdered, someone must now, at this very moment, be contemplating my murder as well!

8

As I sat contemplating this new realization, Walter came into the room. He greeted me with an ironic smile. 'My cousin is rather angry with you,' he said.

'Ellen?' I sighed. 'Yes, I suppose she is. I disturbed Aunt Lydia.'

'I suppose she was back on her wedding plans,' he said. To my astonishment, he had been drinking already, and none too lightly either.

'As a matter of fact, she did talk about marrying someone,' I admitted. In all my anxiety I had not really paid much attention to what Aunt Lydia had been saying.

Walter chuckled and went across to where some decanters were out on a tray. He poured himself a generous glass of what looked to be brandy.

'Her fiancé,' he explained, drinking thirstily. 'She was engaged once, to some tramp that the family disapproved of.'

'She never married him?' I found it

surprising that a woman as strong willed as she could have been persuaded from doing as she wished.

'Never had a chance to. Her brother — Jeffrey's father, that is — made her a prisoner in the house, literally. By the time he gave her freedom back, he had managed to buy off her suitor with a cash settlement and sent him on his way.'

'How dreadful,' I said, shuddering at the thought of such treatment. 'He must have been a thoroughly merciless person.'

'We generally refer to him as dominating,' Walter said. 'It's true, though, he had things pretty much as he wanted them.'

I thought of how that experience had weighed upon Aunt Lydia's mind so that even now she hearkened back to it. And Jeffrey must have been equally under his father's power. What legacy had he left them in grief and tragedy?

I stood; there were things I must attend to. 'Tell me, where would I be likely to find Guy Delane at this hour of the day?'

'You'll find him at the factory, almost any hour of the day. Hasn't anyone explained to you, he's the eager beaver of the clan? He keeps Rome burning while the rest of us fiddle.' He giggled at what he considered his wit.

'I haven't been to the factory yet,' I said. 'Perhaps you can tell me how to get there?'

'If you're driving, you've only got to follow the road into town. It's right on the edge of town, just about the only thing of any importance to see.'

I hesitated thoughtfully. I had never learned to drive. Probably I could find someone about the place to drive me, but I preferred going on my own.

'Is it far?' I asked. 'If I meant to walk, that is.'

'About a mile and a half, if you cut over the hills,' he said, in a voice that indicated he thought that rather too far to walk. 'Past the old convent. Follow the trail around the lake, and over the big hill. From the top of that you can see it in the distance.'

A mile and a half was not particularly far for me; I was accustomed to doing a lot of walking. Moreover, it would be a welcome change to be out of this gloomy house with all its ghosts and shadows from the past.

I took a jacket, as it was already late afternoon, and it would probably be evening by the time I made it back. Leaving the house behind me, I set out.

I had wanted, at first sight of La Deuxieme, to visit the ruins of the old convent. It was this structure, after all, and its history, that shadowed everything here. But this was my first look at it.

It was all in all rather disappointing. Of course, so much time had passed that much of what had remained after the tragedy of the French sisters must simply have rotted away. From the path I could see only the remnants of the old walls and some scattered heaps of rubble. It looked less romantic than one would have expected. Perhaps, I thought, at closer range they would be more interesting, but I hadn't time just now to explore the ruins. I wanted to be sure of seeing Guy Delane when I arrived at the silverworks. There would be time later, or some other day, to examine what was left of the convent.

The path led me to the lake, and then about it. I paused for a moment at the point where it passed nearest the water. There were rushes and tall weeds leading down to the water, and I could see that under its murky surface the lake was thick with plants of one sort or another. It must have been about here that Jeffrey entered the water — or was taken in.

I shivered, although it was still warm, and hurried on.

Walter's directions proved reliable. When I mounted the taller of the hills, I saw a rambling structure in the distance that I took to be the silverworks. It looked quite near, but I knew that the distance was deceiving.

I guessed that the overall distance from house to factory was closer to two miles, but I did not mind that distance.

Guy Delane did not keep me waiting when I arrived. The young man who guarded the door, cool at my initial appearance, became all courteous attention when he learned who I was. He led me to what he said was Mr. Delane's office, and went in search of his general manager. While I waited, I looked around. Guy did not waste any of the money he earned on luxurious offices. This one was business-like and crudely furnished. It also looked as if he did not spend a great deal of his time in it.

'My dear cousin,' Guy greeted me as he came in. He made a slight bow. 'I must express my sorrow at your sudden bereavement.'

I had, remembering him, begun to feel more kindly toward him. I admit it, he exercised a considerable charm; there was an exciting magnetism about him that stirred a woman's blood.

At sight of him, however, my previous impatience came back to me. He looked not at all as if he felt sorrow; rather, I had an impression that he was mocking me.

'Thank you,' I said, more stiffly than I had intended. 'I thought I ought to come to see you as soon as possible,' I said in a more business-like manner. 'I'm aware that you've been managing the business; I understand you've done quite well by it, in fact. I merely wanted to give you my blessing to continue doing so. I don't know what will be needed in the way of official documentation, but for the moment I seem to be the one to decide.'

'What a head you have for business,' he said, 'even to have thought of such a thing at so sad a time.'

I detected a note of reproach in his voice. 'It was called to my attention by a visit from a Mr. Lescott,' I said coldly. 'There was some matter he wanted to settle, that he brought to me. I thought it much more reasonable to refer him back to you. It seemed I needed first to give you carte blanche to continue as before.' I picked up the jacket I had put across a chair. 'So, you have it. Now, if you'll excuse me.'

'As long as you're here,' he said, in a slightly less condescending tone, 'perhaps you'd care to look over the operation? After all, it belongs to you now.'

'Frankly, I doubt that I would understand more than a fraction of what I saw. I think it best if the birds stick to their nests, and the rabbits to their burrows.'

'And which,' he asked, 'do you consider yourself?'

'Not a rabbit, I think,' I replied. 'They seem to frighten easily. I do not.'

He saw me to the door. 'Did you drive?' he asked.

'I walked,' I informed him.

'I can have someone take you back if you like?'

'And neglect my business?' I asked caustically. 'You've given me credit for being a hard businesswoman, Mr. Delane. Perhaps you should treat me as one.'

We parted on those cold words.

9

Although it was well along toward evening, the sky was still light, and the sun was still drifting toward the horizon. Coming over the hill on my way back to the house, I saw the old convent from a different view. I was suddenly struck by its appearance. From above, with the evening shadows playing upon its ruins, it looked as romantic and mysterious as I had originally imagined it.

I had time for a brief look at it, and could still make it back to the house before dark. I did not care to be out at night in an area I did not know — particularly not with the fear in my mind that a murder had been committed here, near this very spot in fact.

The shadows had lengthened by the time I reached the crumbling walls, and I saw that my visit would indeed have to be a brief one. I even considered putting it off for another day; but in the end, I approached and entered the confines of the old structure through an opening in one wall. A gate of some sort had apparently stood here once.

The structure must have been partly of stone, partly of wood. The walls that remained were of stone, held together with what might have been a type of clay. I was surprised to see that some of the wood still remained after all these years. The beams had been massive, although much had rotted away by now. Some of what remained was charred; a grim remainder of the tragedy that had occurred here.

I followed a corridor, now overgrown with weeds, between two walls, and came into what had been an interior court. It too was overgrown, but the stones that had covered the ground still remained among the weeds. The broken walls surrounded me.

I stood, gazing about, and tried to see it as it had looked when new. For all the crudeness of their lives, the sisters had succeeded in building what must have been a handsome structure. How beautiful it must have looked to the weary travelers who came upon it, mounting that hill as I had done, grown accustomed to seeing nothing but wilderness — and there in the valley, a splendid house waiting to welcome them. Perhaps smoke curled from the chimneys, and there may have been flowers blooming about it — certainly the wildflowers would have crept back about the place after a year or two, as they had since. The sound of singing may have carried to the hilltop; perhaps even the scent of food cooking.

There had been that other night, though, and suddenly my imagination brought that to life. I saw the flames rising to the sky, the air thick with smoke. The singing became screams of terror and agony, people trying to flee, confused in the night and the smoke; the walls crumbled . . .

It was too real to me, too horrible. I said 'Oh,' aloud and shook my head to dispel these visions. I turned to leave. It was almost night. The sun was out of sight, and the sky had begun to gray.

The vision lingered. Behind me, the wall really was crumbling, swaying. I cried out, and jumped back, just barely in time. A large section of the wall came crashing down upon the spot where I had been standing!

I stared in horror at the dust drifting upward into the evening. Had I not turned just when I did, in time to see the wall collapsing, I would have been crushed beneath the weight of those stones. I would probably be dead; certainly badly hurt, unable to move.

How had the wall fallen? There was no wind. Nothing had happened to make it fall, after standing all this time. Unless . . . unless someone had made it happen.

As angry as I was frightened, I ran about the part of the wall still standing, enough to conceal a man. There was no man there, only the walls of stone, the fallen timbers, and the weed-covered paths that had once been the halls of the convent.

Had someone been there, someone with time enough to run away when the accident failed to harm me? I went along the path, around a corner in the path — and I saw my man.

Guy Delane stood fifteen feet away.

'Hello,' he said, coming toward me. 'I thought I saw you come in here. Hey, what's the matter?' He stopped in front of me.

I must have looked as pale as a ghost; certainly I was trembling. I said nothing.

'Are you all right?' he asked.

'Shouldn't I be?' I managed to say.

'I heard a racket as I was approaching. And you look like you've seen a ghost.'

'One of the walls collapsed,' I said, watching his face for a reaction. 'It very nearly collapsed on me. I saw it just in time to get out of the way.'

'Good Lord,' he said. He certainly looked surprised, and alarmed. He came closer and put a steadying arm about me. Despite myself, I welcomed it, leaning weakly against him. In my anger at the possibility that someone may have tried to kill me, I had not realized how truly frightened I had been. Now my legs felt as if they were made of rubber.

'Show me where it happened,' he said.

I took him back to the spot. There was nothing to see, actually, but another pile of rubble. Another, that is, because there were other piles of rock and clay just like this one, where other parts of walls, weighted with years, had fallen. They had surely fallen of their own accord, with no need of anyone to push them. *You are letting your imagination run away with you*, I said to myself, trying to regain composure.

Guy bent and looked at the place from which the rocks had fallen. He straightened, looking concerned. 'This place is all crumbling,' he said. 'It isn't safe at the best of times. They should have warned you about prowling around back here by yourself, especially with night falling.'

'I don't suppose it occurred to anyone that I'd try it,' I said, managing a feeble laugh. 'It just occurred to me on the way home.'

'Come on,' he said, taking my arm. 'I'll see you safely home.'

A thought flashed through my mind. 'But what are you doing here anyway?' I asked.

He met my questioning gaze openly. 'Coming after you,' he said. 'To apologize. I behaved badly. I had no right to behave as I did toward you. I'm afraid I'm sometimes thoughtless. I hope you'll forgive me.'

He said all this with such sincerity that I could not refuse to forgive him. 'Of course,' I said. I must confess too, I was happy that the sardonic, mocking side I had seen was not all there was to him.

He took my arm again and led me out of the convent. It was night now; darkness had fallen with the swiftness of spring, catching us unaware despite its long coming.

'There's been a great deal of bitterness between the branches of the family,' he said as we went. 'I don't know whether Jeffrey told you anything about it?'

'A little,' I said.

'I won't rehash it for you now,' he said. 'But sometimes I resent being treated like the poor cousin, the country mouse as it were. And Jeffrey seemed always to end up with the best of everything. I'm not ashamed to admit that I have a jealous streak in me that sometimes surfaces.'

I made no reply to this. I was afraid to believe that it meant what I thought it meant. I don't know how he interpreted my silence, but he too fell silent. We walked that way until we had come to the house.

At the door, he came to a stop. 'I'll leave you here,' he said. Then, after a moment, he went on, 'I was never particularly fond of Jeffrey, and I won't be a hypocrite and pretend that I was. He was too weak for my tastes in a man. But I am sorry for what happened. I'm sorry because I think for the first time in his life Jeffrey had a chance. I think if he had lived, you might have made a man out of him.'

I was flattered by the remark, but I could not in fairness let Jeffrey go undefended. 'Perhaps if you had known him a little better,' I said, trying not to sound as if I were scolding or picking a fight, 'you'd feel differently. He wasn't nearly so spineless as you think him. We met because he risked his life to save mine. Had it not been for him, I would have drowned.'

There had been an unstated bond between us during our little stroll, as if we sensed a rapport that needed no explanation, but my defense of Jeffrey, while it did not provoke him, seemed to sever that bond.

'Again, I'm sorry,' he said, somewhat more formally. 'I forget, he was your husband. I have no right to criticize him to you.'

He started away, then turned back to say, 'Good night.'

'Good night,' I replied, but he was already disappearing into the darkness, walking at a fast, purposeful pace. I stared after him. He was certainly the most exciting man I had ever met, there was no use denying that.

I could not help thinking, this was twice that Guy Delane had been close at hand when what appeared to be a dangerous accident had occurred. There was the shooting incident at home; Jeffrey had thought that not an accident, but an attempt on his life. And only Guy, of all the family, had been within hundreds of miles of the place — at least so far as I knew. And tonight I had come close to being killed or badly hurt by the collapse of an old wall; again, Guy had been close at hand.

Coincidence?

There was no love lost between the two branches of the family. Guy wanted La Deuxieme. Jeffrey had told me that. Aunt Lydia had said that Guy and his mother would stop at nothing to gain control of the estate. Guy had himself told me that he resented being the family's 'poor cousin.'

I was mistress of La Deuxieme. If Guy wanted it, he would have to deal with me. He would have to wrest it from my hands if he could.

Unless, of course, I were to die, preferably in an accident of some sort.

There was, however, yet another possibility. I was, so far as he knew, a widow. If he were to marry me, he would have La Deuxieme.

That was thinking awfully far ahead. Nothing he had said even suggested that he had that thought in mind.

Still, there had been a great and sudden change in his behavior toward me. He had come after me rather quickly to offer his apologies. He had treated me with a new and intriguing charm. Was it only, as he had said, that he had behaved badly, from an impetuous nature, and had realized it afterward, and so sought to make amends? Or were his motives more subtle than that?

I let myself into the house. The lights gave me no sense of welcome. This was no haven for me against the night.

10

There was Jeffrey's funeral to be considered. In the morning I consulted with the undertakers who came from town. Because I knew in my own heart that I had no right to make the decisions that had to be made, I called in the family and deferred as much as possible to their wishes. They seemed grateful for this, and my conscience was somewhat easier.

There seemed no reason for delay and, as the family wanted the ceremonies held quickly, we agreed that they should take place the following day. The services were private, for the family, and of course the Forrests had their own graveyard.

As fate would have it, I had a black outfit with me. I thought, as I donned it, how different the occasion was from what I had imagined when I bought it. How could I have guessed that, less than a week after its purchase, Jeffrey would be dead, and I would be at his funeral in the role of his widow?

Unlike the movies, in which funerals seem always to take place in the rain, the day dawned clear and warm. Summer was just around the corner, and its promise was everywhere. I felt guilty deriving so much pleasure from the golden sunshine and the scented breezes.

The family was together for the occasion. While the minister droned on, I found myself stealing glances at the people about me. One of them may have been responsible for the funeral taking place. One of them might even now be plotting to send me to my grave. I studied them in turn, trying to make some guess as to which of them it might be.

Ellen, of course, was an obvious choice. She had the Forrest backbone and spirit, more of it than Jeffrey had had. But could she have drowned her brother? I doubted it; Jeffrey had been physically strong enough. Of course, had he been drugged, or somehow tricked into the water . . .

Walter was sober this morning. It would be easy to dismiss him as a drunken fool, but he was no fool. His drunkenness did not entirely conceal a clever mind. And he had shown, on the morning of Jeffrey's death, that he could take command of a situation if need be.

Ellen's son, Paul, was not above suspicion. Whatever his mother inherited, he would be in line to inherit as well. He was strong and young, and obviously resented the lesser role that he played in family affairs.

Aunt Lydia was not at the funeral. She had slipped into her incomprehensible chatter about weddings and family quarrels and seemed completely unable to grasp what was taking place. In any event, she was hardly a suspect in Jeffrey's death; she had been too fond of him, and she herself wanted to learn who had caused it.

Except for the servants, that was all of our household.

Across the open grave from us were Guy Delane and a woman who was obviously his mother. He had nodded to me in greeting, but had not come to say anything.

How I would have liked to eliminate Guy as a suspect. But while my heart told me he was not a murderer, my reasoning mind said that he was the one of all these people with the most motive, the most opportunity.

What of his mother? I knew nothing of her but what I had heard from others. What I saw suggested that I had heard the truth. Despite her obvious years, she looked formidable. She was tall and gaunt, and stood with a soldier's ramrod straightness. I looked up once to discover that she was watching me, her eyes seeming to look right through me. Startled and discomforted by her gaze, I nodded in greeting. She seemed not to notice the gesture, but looked down instead. I felt rebuffed, and annoyed that she should treat me so coldly. I felt too that here would be a dangerous enemy. And for all that I knew, she was my enemy already, even though I had never met her.

There was no one else, except for the minister, and Mr. Lescott, who had come out of courtesy.

I wished that I had loved Jeffrey, that I could have felt more grief when it was ended. I could not even really feel that it was ended. I felt that I was waiting for whatever was to happen next.

It happened that very night, as it turned out.

We were a subdued group that evening. I felt more than ever an interloper, intruding upon what should have been a private grief. I found this guilt oppressive, and soon after dinner I excused myself and went upstairs.

I stopped at Aunt Lydia's room. She was the only person in the house whom I could truly regard as an ally, and since enlisting my support, she had not been coherent at all. I could not ignore the fact that I was placing a great deal of faith in the fears of a woman who, at the present, could not even remember who I was, or that Jeffrey was dead.

'I want to see Jeffrey,' she demanded of me when I came into her room.

'Jeffrey's gone,' I said, somehow hoping that the message, couched in that cautious phrase, might strike an understanding chord somewhere in her mind, but she gave no indication that she knew what I meant.

'I want to see him at once,' she said. 'Send him up at once when he returns.'

'I will,' I said sadly. I plumped her pillow for her, filled her water glass with cold water, and went toward the door.

'Who are you, anyway?' she demanded of me. 'I don't know you.'

'I'm Liza,' I said, coming back to the bed so that she could study me again. When she showed no sign of recognition, I added, 'Jeffrey's wife.'

She stared hard at me. For a moment I thought her mind had cleared again, that she recognized me and remembered all that had transpired. Then, as if a curtain had only been drawn aside for a moment, then allowed to fall across the glass again, she said, 'Send Jeffrey to me as soon as he comes in.'

I sighed, and promised I would.

* * *

I woke from my sleep with a start. For a moment I could not think what had awakened me. Then, from some subconscious well of knowledge came the awareness that I was not alone. Someone was in my room with me.

I opened my eyes, lying perfectly still. For a few seconds I saw nothing but blackness. Then gradually I began to make out a shape hovering over me, an outline of white against the room's darkness. A woman in white was standing by the bed. I could not see her face; it was in the shadow cast by the cowl of her outfit. After a moment, I realized that her garb was that of a nun.

I gasped aloud, forgetting my fright, and raised myself up from my pillow. Even as I did so, the figure had moved away from the bed. She went swiftly, silently toward the door. Then, pausing there, she turned back and gestured toward me, as if asking me to follow her.

I hesitated for a second. In that time, she had disappeared into the hall. I sprang from the bed, determined that I should know the meaning of this intrusion. I ran across the room, and into the hall.

The white robed woman was nowhere to be seen.

I went to the end of the hall to peer

down the stairs, and then to the steps at the rear that went down into the servants' quarters. There was no sign of the intruder. I stared the length of the hall. All of the doors were closed. She might have darted into any of these rooms. No lights gleamed to indicate that anyone was awake in any of them.

I nearly sounded an alarm, rousing the household to tell them of the incident and attempt to learn what, if anything, they might know. I did not, however. The family had lost its head; Jeffrey had been buried just today, and I thought that all but one of them genuinely grieved for him. There was Aunt Lydia to consider too; the excitement would only worsen her condition.

Instead, I went back to my room, taking care to lock the door after myself.

It was not until I was in my bed again that the significance of what had just occurred came to me. I had seen one of the ghostly nuns of whom I had heard. The nuns of La Deuxieme, who still haunted this place, had come to haunt me.

11

Although I slept with one eye open, as it were, I was not again disturbed during that night. I woke in the morning with a disquieting sense of fear. It was one thing to have danger as an abstract; it was another to face tangible realities — walls collapsing, ghostly nuns prowling about my room.

At breakfast I told the family of the incident in my room. 'I'm afraid I saw one of the legendary nuns of La Deuxieme,' I said, laughing lightly to show that I did not attach much importance to the incident. 'She came to visit me in my room last night.'

'I've always thought they were the figment of some overworked imaginations,' Ellen said. 'Of course the family history abounds with tales of them, but I believe in what I can see and feel, and not in disappearing wraiths.'

'Wraith or human, there was certainly

something in my room last night,' I said, a bit piqued at her attitude. 'Something real.'

'Did you touch it?' Paul asked.

'No,' I admitted a bit reluctantly. 'But I saw it with my own eyes, and followed it out into the hall.'

'Where did it go then?' Paul asked.

I had to admit, 'It disappeared.'

Mother and son exchanged amused glances. 'The theory regarding such ghosts,' Ellen said, as if she were explaining to a backward child, 'is that the mind creates them as a sort of flight from reality. When one has been distressed, or is under an emotional strain — perhaps there has been an accident that is frightening — it is easier to create a world of spirits, over which one cannot be expected to have control, then to contend with the world of reality which, at such times, seems too much to cope with.'

'You're suggesting, in other words, that I imagined the whole business,' I said.

She shrugged. 'You've had a great emotional strain: the marriage, coming here to strange surroundings, Jeffrey's death, that accident in the convent a couple of days ago, the responsibility of this estate. I shouldn't wonder that your mind conjures up a fantasy or two.'

Walter had said nothing. 'Do you think the nuns are only a fantasy?' I asked him.

He shrugged and said, 'How should I know? Any of the family will tell you that I frequently see things that aren't there, although frankly I haven't seen any French sisters. Of course, what would they want with a reprobate like me?'

I found Ellen's view of the matter annoying and depressing. At the same time she had said some things that made sense. She had been quite right in enumerating the emotional upsets that I had had in the last several days. And it was entirely possible that one's mind might react by conjuring up flights of fancy. Perhaps my fears regarding Jeffrey's death and the danger here at La Deuxieme for me were nothing but that, the escape mechanisms of a troubled mind.

I did not believe in ghosts any more than Ellen did, but I believed La Deuxieme was haunted by its past; I suppose in a sense a house may absorb tragedy, as some houses absorb evil. But the figure in my room had not been a centuries-old French nun, I felt certain of it. It had appeared all too human.

I thought that it had been done to frighten me, to drive me away from La Deuxieme. Later in the morning the housekeeper, Marie, added to that impression. She had come to clean my room. She did not often engage in conversation with me. I had counted as futile my hope of striking up a friendship with her and had settled on the possibility of keeping her neutral. I avoided antagonizing her in any way, and tried to be as friendly as possible toward her. If I should ever have to call upon her for help I would have to rely upon intrinsic human nature, and not upon her affection for me.

On this occasion, however, she struck up a conversation. 'You saw one of the nuns?' she said in what was half question, half statement of fact.

'Yes,' I admitted, guardedly. 'Ellen thinks I imagined it.'

'Maybe she wanted to save you

worrying,' Marie offered, working while she talked.

The remark seemed weighted to suggest something that had not been said. 'Why should I worry?' I asked.

'There's a legend about seeing the ghosts.'

She obviously meant for me to pry the information out of her. Perhaps it gave her a sense of importance. I swallowed my impatience however and asked, 'What does the legend say?'

She turned, fixing her dark, gypsy eyes on me, and said, 'Whoever sees them is fated to die.'

She said it so boldly, all the while looking at me with those great eyes, that I instinctively drew back in fear.

The next moment she smiled, pulling back the corners of her thin mouth, and said, 'Of course it's only a story.'

She gathered up her cleaning things and left on that grim note.

Afterward, I was more than ever convinced that the entire incident had been staged to frighten me. Perhaps whoever had done it thought that I already knew the legend. It angered me that anyone should play the fool with me.

It frightened me too, however. Whichever way one believed — ghost or human trying to frighten me — I had been warned, either by a murderer or by a visitor from beyond the grave, that I was slated for death.

I suppose someone more sensible would have heeded the warning and left, but I was less frightened of death than others, because I had lived so much of my life in his company. And I had a stubborn determination to see something through once I had begun it. No, I would leave La Deuxieme when I felt ready, and not because I had been panicked into it. They'd need an army of nuns to scare me off.

That same afternoon, a servant came from Hamlyn Hall, the nearby Delane home. He brought me an invitation from Margaret Delane, Guy's mother, to come to lunch at Hamlyn Hall the following day.

My impulse was to decline. I was frightened of the power I had sensed in that woman. I was frightened too of the power, of a different sort, that Guy exercised over me. And I could not forget that the Delanes, of all the clan, were the ones most likely to try to take La Deuxieme from me.

If the latter were true, however, then it behoved me to get to know them better, to learn all that I could about them. If they were my enemies, then I ought to size them up.

In any event, as Jeffrey's widow, I could hardly refuse. I had not yet met the woman, fate having arranged things as it had, and she was a relative of Jeffrey's.

I sent the servant home with the message that I would come at twelve the following day.

12

I was as nervous over my visit to Hamlyn Hall as I had been over my coming to La Deuxieme. I was conscious that for perhaps more than one reason I was to be 'looked over.' And if I meant to learn much about those members of my 'family,' then I had double reason for being on my toes.

It was not far to Hamlyn Hall, and with Ellen's directions I set off the next morning. I went in the opposite direction from what I had taken to the silverworks, and had to go about the same distance. This walk took me through the woods that I saw from my window. It was a pleasant path; the air was sweet with the scent of flowers, the grass underfoot lush and green. The trees, heavy with leaves, rustled with every breeze, and birds filled the morning with their songs.

I emerged from the woods to see Hamlyn Hall atop a hill before me. I paused to look at it for a moment. It was smaller than La Deuxieme; but where that place for all its beauty seemed to jar the sensibilities, Hamlyn Hall looked as if it belonged where it was. It was gabled and turreted and multi-chimneyed, and even with my anxieties, it gave off an aura of hospitality.

As I came closer, I saw that Hamlyn Hall was much better cared for than La Deuxieme. Someone — Margaret Delane, perhaps? — had planted neat, colorful beds of flowers — pansies and larkspur and columbine danced in the faint breeze. The paint on the house was fresh, the hedges carefully trimmed.

La Deuxieme was for picture books of great houses, but Hamlyn Hall was a place in which one wanted to live. The Delanes might be formidable, but I got the impression they took more pleasure in the art of living than did the Forrests.

I was met at the door by the servant who had called on me the day before and taken in almost at once to the sitting room where Margaret Delane waited.

'Welcome to Hamlyn Hall,' she greeted

me. 'I see that you walked over. Most of the people from that house find it an effort to get from one room to the next.'

'I enjoy walking,' I replied. 'And I'm pleased to be here. I've heard a great deal about you.'

'None of it good, I'm certain of that,' she said. 'I'm sorry about Jeffrey, and that I didn't get to meet you sooner. Now, with that out of the way, let's sit down, please. I thought we'd have a glass of wine before we ate, if that is acceptable to you?'

It was a question, but delivered in a manner to suggest that only one answer was acceptable.

'Yes, of course,' I replied. We had seats. She made no effort to conceal the fact that she was looking me over. The maid came, brought us wine in delicate crystal glasses, and left.

Mrs. Delane seemed satisfied with her examination of me. 'Yes,' she said, nodding. 'My son said you were lovely. He was right about that. He also said he thought you had backbone. You must feel very out of place where you are now.'

I couldn't help smiling; although her manner was frank, it was refreshing. 'It's still quite strange for me.'

'How is Lydia?'

'Not very well,' I said sadly. 'Her mind is wandering again. I gather it happens from time to time.'

'She was a fool not to go when she had the chance,' Margaret said. Then, changing the subject so abruptly that it caught me off guard, she asked, 'Did you marry Jeffrey for his money?'

'No,' I answered simply.

'You knew he was wealthy, did you not?'

'It would be difficult to ignore the fact,' I said. She watched me closely as we spoke; it would not be easy to deceive this woman. I felt she would put a high premium upon honesty. Strangely, I found myself wanting her approval.

'You cannot expect me to believe that you loved him,' she said with a look of scorn.

'He was quite charming,' I replied, evasively.

'Oh yes, and good-looking, if you liked that type. But he was a ninny, we may as well be frank. Then, if you did not love him, and it wasn't his money, why did you marry him?'

I had not admitted that I did not love Jeffrey, but it seemed pointless to argue this; she plainly had surmised the truth, and if I pursued it I would only end by admitting that she was correct.

'He offered me more happiness than I had had in my past,' I said. She waited, saying nothing. I went on. 'My life before I met Jeffrey was rather a lonely one. I had spent much of my time in hospitals. I've never had a boyfriend; I've never really had a close friend of any sort.'

I went on to explain in more detail; I told her how Jeffrey and I had met, and what his friendship had meant to me. I tried to be completely honest, at least until I reached the subject of our marriage.

'I told him at the time of his proposal that I did not love him,' I concluded. 'He seemed to think we could be happy anyway. Frankly, I wanted to believe him.'

'I see,' she said, when it was apparent I had finished. 'You're very honest. I like that.'

'Thank you,' I replied. 'I have the impression that you are honest too.'

She smiled at that. 'Most people are frightened off by it. They think me cruel and hard, and I am, I suppose. I was never soft and pretty like Lydia; I had to make do with my mind and my will.'

We had finished our wine. She stood; I followed her example and did likewise. 'My son will be joining us for lunch,' she said. 'Ah, here he is now, exactly on cue.'

Guy came in just then. Each time I saw him I was impressed not just by his looks, but his air of strength and character. Though he could be cruel and unkind and cutting, one felt that he was essentially a just man, demanding of others but of his own self even more.

'Liza,' he greeted — 'I may call you that, may I not?'

I nodded eagerly.

We went into the dining room. Lunch was a hearty soup, with warm bread that must have come straight from the oven to the table, and tarts afterward. It was all quite simple, and quite delicious. I had grown accustomed to the lavish, often tasteless meals at La Deuxieme, which were already threatening to change my dress size. This was more to my liking.

If Guy had been more pleasant on our last meeting than in the past, he was today charm itself. Nor did I have an impression that he was making an effort to be charming. It seemed quite natural to him, so that it was difficult for me to remember that he could be cutting when he was unhappy.

When we had finished our meal, with which we did not hurry, Guy suggested that I might like to see the rest of the property. 'It's not La Deuxieme, of course,' he said, with only a trace of bitterness in his voice. 'But we're rather proud of it.

'I should love to see it,' I said with genuine enthusiasm.

'And I shall excuse myself,' Margaret said. 'You have no doubt noticed that I am not young anymore. I must rest in the afternoons. I shan't try to wait up for your departure, my dear. Guy will see you off. I hope you will come again.'

'I would very much like to,' I told her, and meant it. Of all the members of the

Forrest clan, she was the only one toward whom I could feel truly friendly.

Guy seemed to enjoy showing me around Hamlyn Hall and the surrounding estate. I perceived that, despite his resentments toward La Deuxieme, he took real pride in his home. I saw too what I had noticed on my approach, that Hamlyn Hall was kept up much better than La Deuxieme. I could not help thinking it was a shame Guy was not in charge of the entire estate.

'Hamlyn is nearly as old as La Deuxieme,' he explained as we strolled. 'In fact, it is older than the actual house there — if you remember, that was built upon the structure that the nuns had started, but was finished some years later. This house had been built in the meantime, but it belonged then to another clan. The Forrests in time took it over, along with much of the land in the area.'

'I think if I had a choice I would prefer living here,' I said frankly. I realized at once that it was the wrong thing to say. I saw Guy's face darken.

'Yes, it's a much more comfortable house,' he said. 'But there is a matter of principle.' He let it go at that, and I was grateful. A quarrel or a display of mood would have spoiled an otherwise delightful visit.

I was sorry when the time came for me to leave. I would have lingered on, but I gradually came to realize that Guy had taken time from work to return to the house for this lunch. I was flattered by his attention.

'I hope I've made up for my initial rudeness to you,' he said when I was ready to go. He had walked me to the gate in the low stone fence surrounding the house.

'I'm sure you had your reasons for your behavior,' I said. 'But yes, certainly you've made amends.'

He took my hand. 'It was partly jealousy,' he said. 'I was furious that Jeffrey, who already had so much that I wanted, should have you too.'

For a moment we stood in silence, looking into one another's eyes. Then, abruptly, he released my hand. 'I hope you'll come again,' he said.

'Thank you. I will,' I said. We said our goodbyes, and I started for La Deuxieme, following the path into the woods.

I felt weighted down with frustration. In my mind I said all the things I would have liked to say to him. Yet, how could I say them aloud? How could I, who was supposed to be a widow and grieving for the recent death of her husband, tell another man that I loved him?

13

During the next few days nothing seemed to happen. It was as if we existed in a dream world, or a state of suspended animation. I had a feeling of waiting, but for what I did not know.

I say that nothing happened, yet that is not true at all. There were things that happened that were of great importance. I saw Guy again, nearly every day. Several times I called at the silverworks, and I did let him show me about. It would have been obvious, even had I not heard it before, that his industry and good head for business provided the Forrests with their prosperity. He took justifiable pride in his work.

I visited at his house again, and confirmed my favorable impressions of his mother. I found it significant that in our conversations she had as yet made no reference to her claims upon La Deuxieme, of which she must now consider me mistress.

I thought it was probably tact. I tried to ignore the more sinister possibility, that she did not think I would be a problem for long.

I knew that I was falling for Guy, but he regarded me still as his cousin's widow, and behaved with the utmost decorum toward me. I felt cheated. The deception that I had embarked upon for Jeffrey's sake threatened to deprive me of the one true love of my life. I vacillated, wanting to make a clean breast of things to Guy, and telling myself that I dared not, not until the mysteries surrounding me had been resolved.

There was another change during this period. Aunt Lydia recovered, more or less, from her spell. Ellen came to breakfast one morning to report, happily, that the old lady seemed pretty much herself, and might be joining us for dinner. I was elated too, for reasons of my own. When Aunt Lydia was able to have a serious conversation, I wanted to bring her up to date on all that had occurred.

I wanted another opportunity to judge how sound her opinions were. If, upon talking to her again, it seemed that her fears were the workings of an over-wrought mind, I had made up my mind to tell Guy everything. I was almost certain he would not harm me now. And if La Deuxieme meant that much to him, I was even prepared to carry my charade as Jeffrey's widow to the limits, and give the house to Guy. It would mean a battle with the family, but so long as they believed me Jeffrey's widow, they could do very little.

Aunt Lydia did indeed come down to dinner that evening. She looked pale and drawn, but her conversation was lucid. My hopes lifted, and I looked forward to seeing her the following day without the others around.

As it turned out, I did not have to worry about arranging a get-together; she had the same thing in mind. After dinner she caught up with me in the hall. For just a moment we were to ourselves.

'I want to see you,' she said in a whisper. 'About that nun that came to your room.'

I was surprised that she even knew about that incident. I supposed, though, that someone had been bringing her up to date on the household gossip.

'I planned on coming to your room tomorrow,' I replied.

'No, time is wasting,' she said. She sounded agitated, and I feared she might worry herself into another of her spells. 'Tonight. I'll come to see you tonight,' she said.

Ellen was approaching us, and I could do nothing but say, 'All right,' and let it end there.

Aunt Lydia retired early. When she had gone up to her room, and after an interval sufficient that the others would not suspect I was following her, I excused myself and went to my room. It was only nine-thirty, but I thought Lydia probably would come early.

She had not come by ten o'clock. I took a book of John Donne from the shelf and tried to read, but the words slipped meaninglessly through my head like water through a sieve.

There was still no sign of her at ten-thirty. I put the book aside impatiently. Could Aunt Lydia have forgotten?

She had seemed all right at dinner, but her mind slipped so easily in and out of focus. She was old, too. It was possible she had simply lain down to wait for a time, and had fallen asleep.

There was nothing for it but to go to her room and see if she were asleep.

The house was quiet. The others apparently had retired as well. I went quietly down the hall and tapped on Aunt Lydia's door. There was no answer. I hesitated, not wanting to disturb her if she was asleep. Finally I opened the door as quietly as I could, and looked in.

A lamp had been turned low, so that the room was only dimly lit. Aunt Lydia lay on her bed, still clothed. She looked as if she were asleep, and I nearly went back out and returned to my own room.

But something about the way she was lying jarred. I felt suddenly cold, as if a draft had blown across me. I came into the room and started across it toward her bed.

Long before I reached there, I knew that she was dead.

14

Aunt Lydia's eyes were open, staring with eternal horror at some sight I could not see. Her lips were parted as if she had tried to cry out, and one hand had gone to her throat. She might have died of fright.

Stop it, I told myself, fighting off a wave of hysteria. Although there was no doubt in my mind, I nonetheless took her hand and felt for the pulse that was not there. Her skin was cold. She had been dead perhaps since she had first come up to her room; while I waited, impatient with her, the life had fled her frail body.

I had to summon the others, of course. I started for the hall and then stopped.

What had she wanted to tell me? What had she learned that had been so important she felt I must hear it tonight? Was there some clue here, something visible and tangible that would give me the message for her?

Or had her news been only another ghost?

I looked about the room, trying desperately to call up an image of how it had looked before. Nothing seemed changed; nothing struck me as out of the ordinary.

Except, there was a map opened on her dressing table. My eyes passed over it, then came back. Why a map? Aunt Lydia had surely not been planning any trips. Or had she? Perhaps travel was another of her fantasies.

I went about the bed, to the dressing table. The map had been opened out fully. I picked it up, turning it toward the light.

I don't know what I expected. Perhaps a map of the local area. Perhaps something exotic and foreign. I had certainly not expected a map of my own state of Ohio, with my own, insignificant home town circled on it, in red ink that came, I was sure, from the pen on her dressing table.

Had it any meaning, this map that showed where I came from? It might only have represented Aunt Lydia's curiosity about me. Perhaps she had simply looked it up to satisfy herself of the town's location. She had heard of the place before, of course. Jeffrey had come there on family business. Perhaps this was even Jeffrey's map, on which he had planned his original visit to the area, where he had met me.

I put the map back on the table, and turned again to Aunt Lydia. If only she could have told me its meaning. She could never do that now. I had lost the only ally, however frail she was, that I had in the house. The only friend as well. I was completely on my own now. Whatever secrets this house held for me, I must uncover for myself.

It was a sleepless night for all of us in the house. The local doctor, who was coroner as well, came. Aunt Lydia had died, he informed us, of a cardiac arrest. There was, so far as my discreet questions could ascertain, no evidence of any sort of foul play. No struggle, no violence. If someone had caused her death, they had quite simply frightened her to death. That was possible, of course. Any of the family must have known, as I did not until the doctor pointed it out to me, that the old woman's heart was bad and had been for several years.

It was nearly dawn when I returned at last to my own room and fell into my bed. Despite the turmoil and the anxiety of the past several hours, exhaustion had its way with me. It was after noon when I awoke the next day.

An atmosphere of deep sadness filled the house. We had mourned Jeffrey, of course, but Lydia's death, coming so soon on the heels of that other one, left everyone stunned and overcome in a way that we had not been before.

I had made up my mind that the danger in this house was too grave for me to face alone. I needed someone to trust and with whom to share my fears. Of all the people that I had met since my arrival at La Deuxieme, I had faith only in the Delanes, Guy and his mother. Their motives notwithstanding, I was certain that neither of them would stoop to trickery or murder. They were too direct, too coldly honest. They might fight fiercely to regain what they believed theirs, but they would do so openly and without deceit.

I meant to tell them everything: the truth of my relationship with Jeffrey, that we had never married, and that I was not his widow and heir. I meant to confess as well my fears regarding events at La Deuxieme. I was gambling on their characters and what I felt was their genuine liking for me. Instinct and my heart told me this was right. I tried not to think that if I were wrong, the consequences would be grave.

It was evening before I could discreetly manage to go to Hamlyn Hall. The sun had set, and darkness descended quickly. It caught me in the woods that lay between the two houses, but it was a moonlit night and I had no difficulty finding my way without benefit of the sun.

Margaret Delane looked surprised to see me. It was the time of day when she had her dinner. She came from the dining room bearing her napkin.

'Oh, please,' I said, 'finish your dinner. I'll wait for you.'

'Nonsense, I've just finished,' she said; I did not think it was true. 'Come into the study. I'll have someone bring us coffee.'

We went into the study. It was a comfortable room, paneled in oak and lined with fine old books and paintings. I sensed that it was Guy's room, although his mother seemed very much at home here.

We spoke nothing to one another while we waited for the coffee to be served. She seemed to have realized that my visit was not an ordinary one, and she was not a woman to waste breath in small talk when there were serious things to be discussed.

When we were alone, she answered the question I had not asked aloud. 'Guy is not yet home, I'm afraid,' she said. 'Or perhaps you did not want him to hear whatever you've come to say?'

'I mean for him to hear it too,' I said. 'In time. But I haven't time just now to wait for him. And anyway, if I waited, I might lose my nerve.'

'I would be very surprised if you did so,' she said with a not unfriendly smile.

'You're very kind. But,' I went on, 'I'm

afraid that I've presented myself to you under false colors. I've been living a lie since my arrival at La Deuxieme.'

One of her eyebrows lifted slightly, but she made no remark, waiting instead for me to continue in my own time. Perhaps she had even guessed what I meant to tell her.

'Jeffrey and I were never married,' I said, seizing my courage.

For a moment she was silent. Then, quite abruptly, she threw back her head and laughed aloud. 'I thought it must be something like that,' she said. 'I've known all along that something was wrong in the entire business. You're much too clear-headed a girl to have made a mistake like that.' She laughed again, her shoulders shaking. 'And you've made fools of the whole pack of them. They're sweating in their pillows wondering how to get that house away from you, and all the while it isn't even yours. I can't tell you how amusing I find that.'

'Then you're not angry with me?' I asked, relieved that my news had been taken in this manner.

'Angry? My dear, why should I be angry? You've provided me with an amusing story, and confirmed my opinion of what fools that household are.' She grew sober again, seeming to remember her dignity.

'I think, though, that there's more to the story than this. I doubt that it was only meant as a joke.'

'I'm afraid you're right,' I said.

I took a sip of my coffee and cleared my throat, and began to tell my story. I omitted nothing. She had heard already of my meeting with Jeffrey. I went on to tell of the shooting incident that had frightened him so; of my coming to La Deuxieme; of the fears Jeffrey had expressed regarding his father's death, and his fears for his own life.

'And then he died,' she said when I paused. 'How singular that it should have happened just then. I must confess, I thought it strange, and wondered if it might be something more than an accident. But I thought . . . forgive me, but I had not met you yet; the impression was that you had married him for his money. I heard, from the servants, that you had quarreled. I

thought perhaps you, in some way . . . '
She did not finish the sentence; it was not necessary.

It was a time for frankness. 'You needn't feel apologetic for thinking that,' I said. 'I had my reasons for suspecting that you and Guy might have had a hand in things.' I explained what had made me think so.

'Yes, it certainly would look suspicious from your point of view,' she agreed. 'And yet you've come to me tonight, to tell me all this.'

'I felt you were the only person about here to whom I could turn. You see, I've come to fear for my own life.'

She nodded thoughtfully. 'Yes, that would follow,' she said. 'Go on, tell me the rest of it.'

I continued my dialogue, explaining the accident that had occurred at the convent, of which she had already heard; I told of Aunt Lydia's death, and the map I had found in her room, with my home town circled on it. I even told her of the visit to my room by what seemed to be a ghostly nun.

'You don't believe in prowling spirits?' she asked.

'I don't believe it was a ghost in my room,' I replied.

She was thoughtful for a moment, weighing all that I had told her. I felt relieved to have it off my chest. My fear of her reaction to the story had been groundless, and now for the first time this burden of fear was not mine alone, but was being shared.

'But if all this is so,' she said after a few moments, 'then it is dangerous for you to return to La Deuxieme. You must stay here instead.'

I shook my head. 'No. I thought of that as well. It would hardly do for me, as Jeffrey's widow, to move out of the house. And if we're ever to learn who is behind these things, I'll have to continue that deception. I should be on my way home by now, in fact.'

'I wish Guy were here,' she said. 'Perhaps if I called him at the shop and asked him to come straight home.'

'No, I must return to La Deuxieme,' I said, standing. 'I'm afraid I'll have to leave it to you to explain all this to him. I hope he'll forgive me for my deception as easily as you have done.'

She smiled. 'I suspect he'll do so even more quickly. He has reasons of his own for being happy to hear that you weren't married to Jeffrey, if I know my son.'

I did not pursue that remark. She came with me to the door, insisting that I take a flashlight when she saw that I did not have one.

'When Guy comes home, I'll tell him everything,' she said. 'He'll know exactly what to do. He loves taking command of situations.'

I thanked her and bade her goodnight, and started on my way. I went with a lighter heart than when I came.

It was truly night now, however, and by the time I reached the little wood I was grateful for the flashlight Margaret had given me. I picked my way carefully along the path, uneasy as the shadows of the wood closed in about me. The little beam of light seemed to make the night even darker.

I heard a twig snap. In the stillness of

the night it sounded like the report of a cannon, and I came to a halt, listening intently.

The night, which had seemed so quiet, was now a cacophony of sounds — rustlings, whisperings, creakings. Something scurried through the brush — a fox, probably, or a rabbit. A bird in the branches above me complained about the light.

I began to walk again, faster than before.

Suddenly there she was in the path before me, the ghostly nun, in her robes of white. She drew back from the beam of my light. At the same time, someone moved beside her. I turned the light in that direction, and saw a man in black. He wore a cloak that covered him to his feet, and a hat. Even his face was masked in black. He looked, in that forest darkness, like the angel of death!

We might have stood like that for an eternity; time had lost its meaning for me. Then he began to move toward me, and I saw that in his hand he held a rope, tied in a hangman's noose.

I whirled about and began to run, off the path and into the thickness of the wood. A root caught at my foot, and I went crashing down. The light slipped from my fingers and was gone.

15

There was no time to look for the lost flashlight. Behind me I heard a crashing through the undergrowth. They were coming after me. I scrambled to my feet, running desperately. The branches slapped at me, stinging my arms and my face, tearing my clothes. I cried aloud as I nearly ran into a tree.

I had lost my sense of direction. The woods seemed thicker, the pursuing sounds closer. I ran to the side. The tall grass was like cold fingers reaching out to trip me up, to slow my leaden steps. My eyes filled with tears.

I stumbled again in wet grass, and was stumbling and rolling down a ravine, over and over, until I fell in a crumpled heap at the bottom, gasping for breath.

'Liza!' a voice cried. A figure burst from the underbrush, running toward me.

I screamed and tried to escape, but it was useless. In a moment his arms closed about me, but it was no embrace of death; I looked up into the alarmed face of Guy.

'Liza, are you all right?'

'Oh, Guy, Guy,' I sobbed, clinging to him. 'They were after me. The nun and the man in black.'

I looked around us; there was nothing to be seen but the woods and their trees. 'They're gone now,' he said. 'They must have seen me and been frightened off.'

We remained where we were for several moments, kneeling on the ground, his arms about me protectively. At last my breathing had become normal again; I could think.

'Your mother told you . . . ?' I asked.

He smiled and nodded. 'Part of it, at least,' he said. 'That you hadn't married Jeffrey, and that you thought someone wanted to kill you. That's when I came after you, as fast as I could.'

'I'm glad you did,' I said.

For a moment we were silent, looking deeply into one another's eyes. Then, slowly, his lips lowered to mine.

I have no idea how long that kiss

continued. Time and the world were forgotten. I was in his arms, and I was his.

When at last our lips parted I could do nothing but sob incoherently and bury my face against his powerful chest.

'It's getting late,' he said finally. 'We'd better go.'

He helped me to my feet, and we started from the woods. As we walked, I told him all the details that his mother had not had time to tell him. I spared nothing, not even my fears that it might have been him who wanted me dead. Only in truth could we undo the harm that fear had done. I wanted no guilty secrets between us.

'It couldn't have looked any other way to you,' he said sympathetically, squeezing my arm. 'That's my price for being so arrogant and hard-headed. It's I who should ask you to forgive me.'

We came from the woods and approached La Deuxieme. It seemed so long since I had left it. How could I now return to those gloomy corridors haunted by shadows from the past?

At the same time, I knew that I had to return, to learn the truth. I could never know happiness until I had repaid the debt of my friendship to Jeffrey.

'I don't like the idea of leaving you here, not after what's happened,' Guy said.

'There's no other way,' I said.

'Lock your door when you go to your room, and keep it locked. Tomorrow I'll try to find some excuse for moving into the house so that I can keep an eye on you.'

I thought for a moment. 'So far as anyone knows, I'm mistress of La Deuxieme,' I said. 'I could invite you to stay for a few days. You are the manager of the business. Perhaps you could be helping me put the estate in order.'

'It would cause some friction with the others,' he said.

'And maybe smoke someone out into the open?'

He smiled at the suggestion. 'You've got more nerve than a dozen other people. I knew that when I first set eyes on you. It's one of the things that I loved in you.'

We drew into the shadows by the

house, and he kissed me again, briefly, lest anyone be watching. Then he was gone. I was alone at La Deuxieme. Inside, someone wanted me dead.

I drew my shoulders back and went in.

16

I woke in the morning to the realization that my little misadventure in the woods had left me a bit stiff and sore. I had some scratches on my arm that I had to cover by wearing a long-sleeved dress.

That incident had accomplished one thing, however. I had troubled myself again and again with the fear that I had only been imagining the dangers here, letting my fears carry me into creating threats. Last night's happening in the woods had been real, however, and so was the danger I faced. I was grateful that Guy meant to come to La Deuxieme. Nothing bad could happen to me with him close at hand, I was convinced of that. I only wished he were here now.

There were matters concerning Aunt Lydia's burial that had to be attended to in the morning. I felt deeply despondent by the time that business was over. The others seemed to feel much the same way.

Lunch was subdued.

After lunch the family attorneys came to see me briefly. There was still a question of Jeffrey's will.

'If he had anything written up, we should have it,' the attorney explained to me. 'Of course, since his passing occurred so soon after the wedding, it's likely that you won't be mentioned at all. That's no great problem; as his wife, you are entitled to inherit anyway. We'll only need to prove your marriage.'

I kept my face composed and my voice calm. 'Of course.' I said. 'I haven't truthfully looked through my husband's papers, but I shall do so today, and let you know if I find anything that might be pertinent.'

'Fine,' he said. He and his partner rose, satisfied with that answer, and I bade them both good day.

In my quest to uncover the truth, I had gambled that no one might question my marriage to Jeffrey — at least long enough for me to uncover what had really happened. So far my luck had held, and no one had, but the Forrest family were not going to give up their estate without real proof that I was who and what I claimed.

I did not want their estate, true, but I did want to learn the truth about all that had happened here. And in that goal, time was running out for me. I must very soon provide the attorneys with a marriage certificate, or confess the truth. Once the truth was known, I had little doubt I would be asked to leave La Deuxieme, if not ejected forcibly.

One realization offered some hope, however. I had not given any thought to Jeffrey's papers. Now, thinking about them, it occurred to me that quite possibly they might give me some clue to the events happening here.

He had, between the time of his father's death and my arrival here, taken over his father's big office upstairs. Any papers of interest to me would certainly be there. I went up and prepared to spend the afternoon poring over them.

It did not promise to be an exciting afternoon. There were file cabinets and desk drawers and safety boxes filled with papers and ledgers. There were office and business records, correspondence files, receipts. It would take weeks to examine them all in even a cursory manner. I had no more than a day or two at the very most.

I stood in the center of the room, looking about, and tried to think where I should begin. The company records — ledgers, receipts, and the like — were the most voluminous, and seemed to me to offer the least promise of any discoveries. They would have been gone through before by Jeffrey's father and by auditors. They were not likely to hold any secrets, and if they did they were no doubt too well hidden for my untrained eyes to discover them.

I examined the fronts of the file drawers. The first of them was labeled personal correspondence. The lettering was old, and I assumed that this was correspondence belonging to Jeffrey's father rather than Jeffrey himself. Here there might be a clue; but I felt reluctant to pry into the private life of a man I had not even known.

There was an entire cabinet labeled simply, La Deuxieme. My pulse quickened. Yes, it was La Deuxicme itself that had inspired the passions in these people. La Deuxieme about which had centered tragedy and violence, and bitter anger. If I was to find a motive for murder, it would be here, in the history of this house. I opened the drawers of the cabinet eagerly.

Here was everything I could want to know about the house and its history. There were clippings from magazine and newspaper stories about the house. It was indeed famous. I read a few of these hastily, but they did not add appreciably to what Jeffrey had told me about the place.

There were books and historical documents too that dealt with the history of the area in general. In a folder marked Legal, I found what appeared to be a copy of the original land grant, as well as other documents apparently establishing the ownership of the house. They were all duplicates. The originals, I supposed, would be locked up somewhere, perhaps in a bank vault.

Disappointed with my search so far, I went on to another drawer. This one appeared to be a combination of letters and legal documents. After glancing at a few of them, I realized that these were the record of the claims of ownership that had been made against the place, and the battles that had been fought over that.

I looked through these. I saw letters and affidavits signed by Guy and Margaret. I passed over these. I knew in my heart that they were not my enemies.

There were hundreds of papers. Jeffrey had told me that bitter battles had been fought in attempts to gain control of the estate. But I had not realized how many there had been, or how long and drawn out some of the fights had been. It seemed as if everyone who ever heard of the house had somehow tried to prove himself the rightful owner.

Here, of course, was motive enough for murder, but there were so many letters, so many people involved. How could I know who among them might murder?

It was like looking for a needle in a haystack. I was about to give up the idea of finding anything useful here, when an address on a letter caught my eye. It was from my own hometown.

I brought it out. It was part of a file bearing on one of the lawsuits over the house's ownership. I brought out the entire file.

The letter was indeed from my own town, from a man who, like all the others in these files, had claimed to be the rightful heir to La Deuxieme. There were dozens of letters, to and from the man himself, and to and from lawyers. There were copies of court judgments and affidavits and other legal looking documents. The fight had been a particularly bitter one.

The man making the claim was of French descent. He signed his name Lescaut, and he was a silversmith.

Lescaut — Lescott. Silversmiths, both from the same small town. It was surely too much of a coincidence.

17

I took the file to the big desk that stood in the center of the room and began to read it carefully. It began with a suit filed by Lescaut and a sister, claiming rightful ownership of La Deuxieme and the entire estate, including the silverworks and Hamlyn Hall.

No small ambitions for them, I thought grimly.

It seemed from the papers before me that there had been some basis for the claim. Lescaut was of French descent, an ancestor of the leader of the band of French nuns who had first settled here and built the convent and La Deuxieme. There were copies of documents establishing this relationship.

When the sisters, following the tragedy here, had moved on, Lescaut's ancestors had claimed title to the properties. The French governor had given a grant to one of them, it appeared, but only a few days before the time that the English, now in control of the area, granted it to the Forrests. There had been a dispute at that time, settled apparently when the Forrests gave that Lescaut another piece of property that they owned.

The second chapter of this story began with the appearance of another Lescaut, a grandson, some sixty years later. He too claimed ownership to the estates. Again the Forrests had retained legal ownership and had appeased the claimant with a gift; this time they had given him a salary from the silverworks which they were now operating successfully.

The third chapter began only a dozen years ago, when the current-day Lescaut had revived all this history with his claim. For the third time the affair had been resolved in the courts in favor of the Forrests. This time the Forrests had offered and paid what seemed to me a generous cash settlement.

This Lescaut had not been satisfied, I feared. The file ended there, with the payment of the settlement. I was almost certain the story had not ended there.

I rose from the desk elated. It seemed almost certain that Lescaut was Lescott. Not satisfied with the legal outcome of his efforts, presumably bitter and convinced that he had been cheated, he had set out to wreak vengeance upon the family who held what he considered his property.

I had to be very sure of this before I made any charges, however. It would not be difficult to learn the truth. Lescott was at the factory. I had only to somehow obtain his signature and compare it to the one on file here. Nothing could be simpler. If they were not the same, then this was all only coincidence. I could keep it entirely to myself, and no one would be harmed by false charges. But if they were the same signature, then I had surely found my guilty party.

I took one of the letters from the file and, folding it neatly, put in the pocket of my dress. It was growing late. I took a jacket from my room and set out for the factory, walking swiftly. As I passed the ruins of the old convent, I thought that I might soon be laying to rest the ghosts that haunted La Deuxieme.

I had meant to ask Guy for some document that would bear Lescott's signature. I was certain that there must have been signed agreements covering the old man's work here at the shop. But Guy, I was informed on my arrival, was out at the moment.

In his office, I looked through files and desk drawers for some such agreement. Guy was not, alas, a neat records keeper. I could find nothing.

'Very well,' I said stubbornly, 'I'll have to get the signature from Lescott himself.' I thought for a moment; then I sat at the typewriter in the office and, picking out the letters slowly, managed to type up a document that looked, I thought, serious enough that my wanting it signed would seem reasonable, and yet sufficiently trivial that Lescott would not hesitate about signing it. It was merely an agreement on Lescott's part to negotiate with Guy, as manager, and with me, as Jeffrey's heir, any business matters that had been pending between him and Jeffrey. The legal terms that I had absorbed in the perusal of the documents in the files at the house came into use. The document, when I was finished, had an official ring to it.

I went into the shop to find Lescott. He had been given a section of his own in which to work on his designs. I found him there. He greeted me with his usual courtesy. I tried as best I could to conceal the nervousness I felt.

'I'm sorry to disturb you,' I said when we had exchanged greetings. 'I've been consulting with the attorneys. They thought I ought to get your signature on an agreement.' I gave him the document I had typed up. He looked it over with no expression on his face.

'It's only a formality, of course,' I said, talking more quickly than I should. 'I don't understand it awfully well, I'm afraid. They seem to think they'll need this before any final agreement is drawn up between you and the firm. As I understand it, it gives them the authority to go ahead and prepare the agreements.'

I thought that I had failed in my attempt. He read and reread the document, still with no show of what he was really thinking.

Finally, to my relief, he said, 'Seems to

be perfectly silly, but you know what a nuisance attorneys can be.'

I tried not to look too pleased when he had put his signature to the paper and given it back to me. 'Thank you,' I said, folding it and putting it into my pocket. 'I'm sure you're right, it no doubt is quite silly.'

I left him. I had to restrain myself from racing back to Guy's office, but I was too afraid that Lescott might be watching me go.

Inside Guy's office, I hastily took both the papers from my pocket. My fingers trembled as I unfolded first one and then the other.

The two signatures were the same, I was certain of it, notwithstanding the difference in spelling. Unless I was very mistaken Lescott was Lescaut, who felt that he had been cheated out of La Deuxieme.

I went to the telephone and dialed Hamlyn Hall. It was Margaret who answered.

'No, Guy's just left,' she replied when I asked for him. 'Can I give him a message?'

'No,' I said, disappointed. Then I changed my mind, and said quickly, 'Yes.' My discovery was too important to be known to me alone. And I knew that I could trust Margaret with the information.

'I've learned something very important,' I told her, 'about the man who calls himself Lescott.' Briefly I told her of my discovery.

'Then Lescott is the one behind all that's happened,' she said.

'I'm sure of it. I want to tell Guy of this as soon as I can, of course. If you talk to him, tell him to come to La Deuxieme at once.'

I hung up the phone and left the office, hurrying outside. Now that I knew the truth, I wanted to share it at once with the Forrests. It would mean exposing myself as a fraud, but there was no longer any reason for the deception. And until Lescott had been brought to justice, the danger that I had thought mine alone was a threat to the entire family.

So intent was I upon my purpose that I had travelled half the way home before I even looked back. I had come over the hill, and was approaching the old convent. Here the road came near to the path on which I travelled. A cloud of dust told me someone was coming along the road. As it came near, I recognized the vehicle. It was a battered old pickup truck that belonged to the factory. It had been given to Lescott to drive while he was here; Guy had cleared the arrangements with me himself after Jeffrey's death.

Lescott! It might only be coincidence that he was going to La Deuxieme in such a hurry, but my heartbeat quickened in fear.

He seemed to catch sight of me. The truck came to an abrupt stop, and Lescott jumped from the driver's seat, running toward me.

I stood where I was for a moment, trying to tell myself that he might have some legitimate reason for wanting to see me, that his appearance now did not necessarily mean he suspected that I knew the truth.

He was close enough now for me to see his face, and suddenly I knew that this was no casual meeting. He knew that I had discovered who he was and what he was doing here. On his face was an expression of evil and of hatred.

I sprang into motion with a little cry, whirling about and running. He was between me and the house; I ran in the direction of the ruins. I ran with all the speed of which I was capable and yet it seemed as if I were hardly moving at all. The crumbling walls of the convent crept closer. Behind me I heard Lescott swear aloud.

I reached the walls, running between them. The grass-covered corridors ran between and among the ruins. I rounded a corner, gasping for breath. My lungs were aching; a pain erupted in my chest. I wanted to stop to get my breath back, but even as I slowed my steps, Lescott cried, 'It's no use, I'll get you.'

My eyes darted frantically about, but it was futile. There was no place here that would be safe enough to hide in. Anywhere that I stood he could find me as he came about a wall.

My feet felt as if they were made of lead. I stumbled and nearly fell, catching myself instead on the rough surface of stone beside me. I fell against it weakly, gasping for breath. Perhaps if I remained silent he might go on by; might think I had eluded him.

I listened. He too had stopped apparently. I heard nothing for a moment. I watched the corner where I thought he would appear, the corner about which I had come.

Suddenly behind me he cried, 'Ah!'

I turned, startled, to see him only a few feet away. Between us was nothing but a fallen wall, a heap of rubble. Even as I turned he started to scramble over it.

I ran again, but I knew that I could not escape him; I hadn't the strength left. Years of sickness and convalescence had left me with scant resources for this type of flight.

I rounded a corner and before me an open space of green grass led down to the lake. The lake where Jeffrey had drowned! I had trapped myself, with no way to go back, and nowhere to go before me but into the water.

Even as I slowed my steps, Lescott gave

a cry of triumph and grabbed at my arm. I screamed and yanked free, half running and half stumbling. There was nowhere for me to go but into the water. I felt its cold wetness on my feet; then I was splashing into it, each step an agony. It held me back, slowing me down terrifyingly.

Lescott seized me again. This time I could not break free. I struggled, and we fell into the green water. The bottom of the lake was slimy and thick with growth that twisted about my feet. It was like the hands of some awful underwater monsters seizing me, pulling me down. My head sank beneath the surface and I swallowed water.

For a moment Lescott released his grip on me as he struggled for his own footing in the slippery mud. I gulped air gratefully and tried to splash away from him, but my strength was spent. When he seized me again I could scarcely struggle against him. He seized my throat and slowly, overcoming my faint resistance, he pushed my head down, down, under the water. The sun disappeared and there was only the green tinted darkness, cold and heavy. My body seemed to float free. I grew limp.

This was what it was like to drown, I thought. This was how Jeffrey had gone. I had lived so long close to death, but never before had his presence been so real to me. I thought of all that I had read and heard, and I almost waited for my life to flash before me.

There was only the nothingness of the water. I tried once more to pull his hands away from my throat, but even as I clawed feebly at his wrists I knew that it was useless, that I could never escape that murderous grip.

18

I thought that the end had come for me. There was nothing but the cold dark water and the hands that held me, bearing me down.

Then, suddenly, the hands were gone. I was splashing and bobbing in the water, free. I gasped for air, filling my lungs greedily. The roaring in my ears began to fade.

Guy was there. I saw him struggling with Lescott. The old man fought with the ferocity of an angry tiger, but he was no match for Guy's young strength. In another moment it was over, Lescott subdued and gasping on the sandy bank. He looked too winded to make an escape.

I was still in the water, on my knees. Guy came to me and helped me up. 'You all right?' he asked.

I managed a feeble nod. My throat was sore from trying to draw in air and bruised from Lescott's strong fingers, but

I was grateful to be alive. Never had life been so wonderful a thing to me as in those moments when I had thought I was losing it.

Guy removed his belt and used it to fasten Lescott's hands behind him. 'So it was you,' he said to the old silversmith. 'I should have realized. Lescaut, the man who thought La Deuxieme should be his.'

'And it should be,' Lescott said angrily. 'Your family cheated us of it. But I meant to have it. I've thought of nothing for ten years but having my revenge.'

'And you've stopped at nothing,' Guy said. I knew that he was trying to draw a confession from the old man. Lescott was too angry to use caution. He spoke with all the bitterness of his years of frustration.

'You murdered my uncle,' Guy accused him.

'Yes, and your fool cousin,' Lescott said. 'It was easy to have him drugged and bring him here in the night. I had only to hold him under the water until his lungs were filled.'

I shuddered as I thought of how Jeffrey

had died. I had nearly died the same way myself, at the same hands. Poor dear Jeffrey, sleeping, never knowing that he was drugged, that he was being carried from the house, held beneath the water's surface — it was a ghastly picture.

'And I'd have done away with you, too,' Lescott cried, as if reading my thoughts. 'If he hadn't interfered.'

'I got back to the shop just after you left,' Guy said to me. 'I called Margaret about something else, and she told me what you had discovered. I went to look for Lescott. When one of the men told me he had left in a hurry, I was certain he must be after you. I came over the hill in time to see him drag you into the water. I was afraid I was too late.'

'You nearly were,' I said. 'Another minute and I'd have been a goner.'

We went up to the house, Lescott walking dejectedly before us. Ellen was in the hall when we came in. She looked appropriately startled. We must have made quite an entrance — Lescott with his hands bound and a look of undis- guised loathing on his countenance; I with my clothes dripping wet; Guy almost as wet as I was, and clearly in command of the situation.

'What on earth . . . ?' Ellen exclaimed. Her surprised cry had brought Walter and Paul into the hall as well. They stared at us.

'Meet Mr. Lescott, pretender to the throne of La Deuxieme,' Guy said. 'And murderer of your brother Jeffrey; and almost murderer of Liza. Paul, call the sheriff; tell him to send someone out to pick this guy up.'

Paul went hastily to do Guy's bidding. I was amused to see how quickly even he, who pretended to despise Guy, hurried to obey Guy's commands. Guy was a man who exuded authority.

We went into the sitting room; Guy ordered Lescott into a chair where he could keep an eye on him. Paul was back in a moment.

'The sheriff's coming right over,' he said.

'Now,' Ellen said, looking from one of us to the other, 'I think you owe us some sort of explanation.'

'It's a long story,' Guy said, looking at me. 'And I think maybe you ought to begin it.'

I nodded. There was no longer any reason to continue my deception. 'In the first place,' I said, 'you may as well know that I'm not the heir to La Deuxieme, as you have thought. I'm not Jeffrey's widow. Jeffrey and I were never married.'

There were murmurs of surprise from the others. 'But why did you lead us to believe . . . ?' Paul asked.

'Jeffrey told you, to begin with. And he begged me to pretend that it was so. He was afraid that he was going to die; that someone wanted to murder him. When he died, I was convinced that his fears had been justified. I continued in that guise in the hope that I could learn the truth.'

'And it nearly cost Liza her life,' Guy interjected.

He took over the explanation in part, explaining who Lescott was, and how he had tried to kill me at the lake to keep his secret safe.

When the story was finished, Ellen said, 'How dreadful. If we had listened to

211

you at the beginning, at the time of Jeffrey's death, an investigation could have begun then. Our stubbornness nearly cost you your life.'

'You couldn't have known,' I said. 'You didn't know about the shooting incident before I even came here. That was Lescott, of course. Jeffrey wouldn't have confided his fears to you, because he thought one of you might be responsible. You didn't have any reason to suspect anything so extreme as murder.'

'Still,' Walter said, 'we were very nearly responsible for your death. I for one am sorry.' The others chimed in, each expressing the same regret.

'And I for one am happy to give you back your home,' I said. 'I've never wanted La Deuxieme, and I haven't enjoyed being its mistress, even if it was only pretend. It's yours again, to deal with as you will.'

Of course they were happy to realize that La Deuxieme was theirs again, and not the property of a usurper, although good manners prevented them from openly showing this.

'But what of you?' Ellen asked. 'You're

more than welcome to stay on here if you like.'

'She has other plans,' Guy said quietly.

'What sort of . . . oh.' Ellen looked from him to me, and began to smile broadly. 'It seems to me that you're downright determined to marry into our family.'

'Only this time,' I said, 'it won't be a pretense, it will be for real.'

The sheriff came a few minutes later. It was necessary to go through the explanations again. He was abashed to think that he had insisted on labeling suicide or accident what he now saw to be murder.

'Maybe I ought to give you a job on the force,' he said to me. 'Looks like we could use somebody with your clear-sightedness.'

'She has a job already, I'm afraid,' Guy told him. 'A full-time position.'

'You'll have to come with me to sign statements,' the sheriff told Guy. 'We'll need statements from the rest of you in due time, especially from you, Miss Durant. But you look all in. Tomorrow will be soon enough for that. The only thing now is to get this fellow booked properly.'

'I'll come with you,' Guy said.

I went with them to the door. 'I'll have to see about things at the shop,' Guy said to me, holding me in his arms. 'And then I'd better get home and bring Mother up to date. I expect she's in a fair lather by now. I think you'd better get some rest, and I'll see you in the morning. All right?'

'Yes, of course,' I assured him. 'For a change I'll be able to sleep without any fear.'

'Until tomorrow,' he said, bending down to kiss me.

'Until tomorrow.'

When he was gone, I allowed Ellen and the family to persuade me to share a glass of wine with them, in a manner of toasting my accomplishments. After that, genuinely tired, I asked Ellen if she would have some warm milk sent up to my room.

'I really ought to change rooms,' I said, pausing on my way upstairs. 'After all, the one I'm in belongs to the mistress of the house.'

'You've earned the right to use it,' Ellen said. 'It shall always be there for you, whenever you want it.'

Upstairs I enjoyed the luxury of a hot

bath, sinking down into the water and allowing it to soothe my aching muscles. When I came from that, wrapped in a warm robe, Marie was just bringing the warm milk on a tray. Even her particularly surly expression could not dampen my spirits this day.

I drank the milk and then, although it was barely evening, put myself to bed. It had been an exhausting day, and I wanted nothing so much as to rest for a time.

Tonight, I told myself, sinking gratefully into the softness of a pillow, *I don't have to worry about any ghostly visitors.* With that thought in my mind, I fell asleep almost at once.

I was mistaken in that belief, though. I woke later with a start. It was dark in the room; I had apparently slept through dinner time; the family had no doubt decided simply to let me sleep rather than waking me.

I decided that I was, after all, more inclined to sleep than to eat. I felt as if I hadn't slept for a week. I turned over in the bed — and there, standing at the side of the bed, was a white-robed figure.

19

For a moment I could not comprehend. At last it came to me — the nuns of La Deuxieme. Twice before I had seen this figure. Once she had come to my room like this in the night. The second time had been in the woods, when she had been with the man in black.

But the man in black had been Lescott; and I thought as I sat up in the bed, that my ghostly nun was equally human.

She did not run away this time, but stood by the bed as if waiting for me to say or do something. I reached for the light and clicked it on.

'Marie,' I gasped, astonished. The cowl of her outfit was drawn far forward. With the light out it had thrown her face in shadow so that I could not see it. Now the light fell boldly on it. It was indeed the surly housekeeper.

She smiled, but there was nothing pleasant in that expression. Suddenly a thought came to me, something that I should have realized before.

'Lescott had a sister,' I said. 'I remember now from those letters. You . . . '

She nodded, chuckling evilly. 'Yes, I am his sister,' she said. 'And the rightful heir to La Deuxieme.'

My mind was racing. I had to think of some way to persuade her to a reasonable view. But my thoughts were not clear; my brain felt cloudy. It seemed as if I could not shrug off the sleep from which she had awakened me.

'Marie,' I said, speaking with some difficulty. 'Of course, it all makes sense now. I should have realized your brother could not have managed everything by himself. He needed someone else, someone inside the house.'

'I've been here three years,' she said. 'It was easy to come here and get a position. I bribed the housekeeper who was here; for the right price, she was willing to quit her job. And the very same day I was here seeking it. They hired me on the spot. And it was I who saw that my brother's silver work was brought to the attention of old Mr. Forrest. How I laughed when he sent his milksop son to persuade my brother to join the mighty Forrest family in their enterprises. Little did he know that we would someday rule them.'

'But you needn't have gone to such lengths,' I said. 'Nor do you need to now. We can work something out, I'm certain.'

I realized that she did not know that I was not mistress of La Deuxieme. The family had not thought to tell her. I hoped that I might appeal to her greed.

'Your brother is under arrest, of course,' I went on. My tongue felt thick and unresponsive. 'I can't undo that. But I can give you a part of the estate. You could be one of the directors of the silverworks.'

'A director,' she sneered. 'We'll own it, my brother and I. When the Forrests are gone, there'll be no one to dispute our claim.'

'Marie, I'm not a Forrest,' I cried in desperation.

'You are in name,' she said. She came toward me menacingly.

I tried to scramble from the bed, but it

was no use. My arms felt as if they were made of lead. My body did not respond to the commands I gave it.

I sank back against the pillow. The light seemed to be coming and going in waves, like a surf breaking upon a beach. Marie laughed again.

Then I realized the truth. 'The milk you brought me earlier,' I said. 'You . . . '

'It was drugged,' she said.

'I'm not a Forrest, not even in name,' I said. I knew that consciousness was fading from me. 'I never married Jeffrey. I've been posing as his widow to learn the truth about his death.'

'You expect me to believe that?' she asked. 'A minute ago you were offering to make me a director of the firm. You're wasting your breath, you little fool. If you had gone away as you were warned, you might have saved your life. Now you'll die with the rest of them.'

'Die . . . ' I fought against the blackness threatening to envelop me. There had to be some way out of this, something I could do. If only she were not here, I felt I could summon the strength at least to rise, but I would never be able to fight against her.

'When I leave here, I'm going to leave the house in flames,' she said, leaning close so that I could not fail to hear what she was telling me. 'The Forrests will be consumed, just as those nuns were consumed. And my brother and I will own everything.'

She was mad, of course. I had no doubt that she would do what she was threatening. And I had no way to prevent it.

'You'll both hang,' I said hoarsely. 'Your brother has been charged with murder already. You might yet be saved, but not if you go through with this.'

'There'll be no one to stop me,' she said. Her face was twisted in an ugly expression that made a mockery of the saintly gowns she was wearing.

She bent over me, her eyes flashing. 'And now,' she said, 'you must sleep. I don't want you screaming and warning the others. I want them to be surprised by the little fire I've prepared for them.'

She took the pillow from the bed beside me and lifted it toward my face.

'No,' I cried, trying to fight her away. She was too strong, and I had virtually no strength left. I could only thrash weakly from side to side as she pushed the pillow down over my face. I could see nothing. I fought for breath but no air could penetrate the barrier that covered my mouth and nostrils. My screams were trapped in my throat.

I fought desperately to push the pillow away, but she held it tightly in place. I could feel life ebbing from me.

Her voice came to me, muffled, through the pillow. 'You little fool,' she rasped. 'It was I who killed the old man. I replaced his drugs with water. It was I who drugged your husband so my brother could carry him from the house and drown him. If you'd been one half so clever as you think you'd have realized these things. And who did you think it was who came to your room in the night, or waited for you in those woods? Did you think there were really ghostly nuns trying to frighten you off?'

She was right about the nuns, my frantic mind thought. She had told me that seeing the nun was an omen, a warning of impending death. And unless I could somehow break free from her, I was going to die here, tonight.

I made a final effort, but it was doomed to failure. I hadn't the strength left.

'The old lady guessed,' she was saying; I heard her as if from far away, her voice fading . . . fading. 'She saw me in that costume and guessed the truth. I would have killed her too, if her heart hadn't given out. I scared her to death, I guess you could say.'

I heard her laugh wickedly. That was the last that I heard. I was imprisoned in darkness that deepened, growing blacker and blacker, until all awareness fled from me and I sank into unconsciousness.

20

I woke slowly, at first unable to recall where I was or what had happened. The darkness faded somewhat, replaced by a flickering light that seemed to come and go, brighter each time, as the tide advances coming in, moving further up the beach with each thrust.

After a long time, I realized what the light was — fire! I struggled to gain full consciousness, but the drug I had been given earlier, and probably the smoke I had already inhaled, made my limbs feel as if they were made of lead, and my thoughts uncontrolled.

I got to a sitting position and somehow got my feet to the floor. The room was filled with smoke that billowed in through the open door. The flames were brighter now. Even as I sat, trying to propel myself into further action, the flames began to lick about the door frame. The heat was incredibly intense.

It seemed an eternity before I was able to get to my feet, clinging weakly to the bedpost. The room reeled and tilted. *I'll never escape from here*, I thought. But stubborn determination returned to me.

Gradually my head cleared. I could stand without the help of the bedpost. But the fire was spreading faster. The entire door was ablaze by this time.

I began to walk, swaying unsteadily. The smoke was overpowering, choking me. I coughed and gagged, and thought I would faint again.

Somehow, I have no idea how much later, I reached the door. I dared not put out a hand to support myself now — the walls and woodwork were flaming.

As I came into the hall the heat was like a slap across my face. I felt as if I had descended into the very pit of Hades. With the flames and my drugged state, I could hardly retain a sense of direction; for a moment I could not remember the way to the stairs.

Think, I ordered myself. *Think, for the sake of your life!*

I remembered then. The back steps

were to my right. They were narrow and closed off. If the fire had spread to there, they would be the most dangerous. The wide front steps were to my left. I went in that direction, stumbling. I put my arm across my face, breathing through the fabric of my nightgown, but every breath brought strangling smoke into my lungs.

I had almost reached the steps when I saw Marie. I could not make out her face, but the white nun's habit stood out in the blackness. She must have stayed behind to die in the blaze. She moved toward me, hands outstretched. She was between me and the stairs.

I had no choice but to go the other way, toward the rear steps. I knew I was too weak to struggle with her. I even doubted that I could escape her.

I had just turned, to make my way to the rear, when I heard the sound of breaking wood. I looked back. Marie was gone, but as I watched, the fire-eaten stairs collapsed down. With a roar and a rush of smoke, they were gone. Marie must have gone with them.

She had saved my life. Another

moment and I would have been on those steps.

I had, perhaps, no more than seconds before the rest of the house would collapse. I ran blindly, bumping into walls that seared my flesh. I thought of the nuns of La Deuxieme. They had died in flames like this; their home crashing down about them. In my dazed state I could almost hear their horrified screams, their cries of agony.

Choking and sobbing, I found the back steps. They were still whole. The flames gleamed from below, shining through the clouds of smoke. For a moment terror held me back, but I must try to descend through that smoke and fire; it was my only hope for survival.

I began to descend. Each step was a new nightmare. The heat rushed up to meet me, like solid sheets of flame. I tried to concentrate upon the steps beneath my feet, tried not to think of the holocaust about me. One step — two steps — three — four — five, stumbling, nearly falling — six . . .

I would never make it. My legs were numb; my feet felt as if they were weighted. I sank to my knees, trying to brace myself against the red-hot wall. Something burst into fresh flames at my feet; in horror I realized it was the cloth of my nightgown. I brushed at it, trying to tear off the part that was burning; my head began to spin.

I'm dying, I thought. *Dying like those frightened women two centuries before me. They've claimed me for their own. La Deuxieme. The second house. Le couvent. Guy. My darling, Guy . . .*

Blackness closed in about me again.

In my delirium I saw the nuns, hovering above me. They seemed to be pleading with me to rise, to make good my escape. I think I tried to move, but I could not. Their frightened faces faded, returned, and faded again.

Guy was there, his face close to mine. 'Liza, darling,' he said. 'Just hold on to me.'

This was no dream. I was in Guy's arms: he was carrying me down the stairs, holding me close to his body for protection. We came to a wall of flame. He was running. Then, suddenly, we were through it, we were outside, and I was drinking in the night air in a rush.

Someone brought brandy, someone else put a blanket about me. Slowly, consciousness came back to me. Guy was there, his arm about me. We were on the lawn. Beyond him, over his shoulder, I could see La Deuxieme, what was left of it, aflame. The flames seemed to reach to the sky. I heard sirens approaching, but they would never be able to save the house. It had been destroyed just as the old convent had been destroyed, and I had nearly been destroyed with it.

'Better?' Guy asked, holding the glass that held the brandy.

I nodded weakly. 'How did you . . . ?'

'The sheriff called me. Lescott had confessed to everything, including the fact that Marie was his sister. As soon as I heard that, I knew you were in danger. I called to warn Ellen, and then started over, but it was almost too late. Marie had already set the house afire. Ellen wasn't able to reach your room through the flames. I had to try to get you out, and the back stairs seemed the only part of the house not yet burning. I started up, and found you unconscious there. We just got out before the walls started collapsing.'

'Marie,' I said, remembering how she had inadvertently saved my life, and lost her own, by frightening me away from the front stairs before they collapsed. 'She's still in there.'

'Oh no, not her,' he said, shaking his head. 'She was just running out when I came up. I caught her in the nun's costume that she used to frighten you.'

'Marie . . . but how . . . ?' I tried to think. She could not have made it down the stairs, I was certain of that. So that had not been her that I saw.

If not her, who? The others had all escaped the house. I was alone there. My eyes had only played tricks on me. I must have imagined that I saw her.

Unless . . . unless I had seen one of the nuns, the ghosts of La Deuxieme. That was incredible; I didn't believe in ghosts and the like.

But something — an apparition, a hallucination — *something* — had saved my life by warning me away from those stairs.

I shook my head. I would never know, of course. And in time the nuns would be forgotten. The legends of La Deuxieme would die with the house. I found myself thinking again of those poor women who had died in that other fire. It had taken almost two hundred years, but at last they would be allowed to rest

'You've lost La Deuxieme,' I said to Guy.

'I've found something far more precious,' he said. His arm tightened about me.

'I have a kitten at home,' I said, knowing perfectly well that it was a silly thing to say; I was feeling the relief, the exhaustion, the drug, the brandy. 'A little yellow kitten, named Hepzibah.'

'She'll love Hamlyn Hall,' he said.

THE END

We do hope that you have enjoyed reading this large print book.

Did you know that all of our titles are available for purchase?

We publish a wide range of high quality large print books including:
Romances, Mysteries, Classics General Fiction Non Fiction and Westerns

Special interest titles available in large print are:
The Little Oxford Dictionary Music Book, Song Book Hymn Book, Service Book

Also available from us courtesy of Oxford University Press:
Young Readers' Dictionary (large print edition) Young Readers' Thesaurus (large print edition)

For further information or a free brochure, please contact us at:
**Ulverscroft Large Print Books Ltd., The Green, Bradgate Road, Anstey, Leicester, LE7 7FU, England.
Tel:** (00 44) **0116 236 4325
Fax:** (00 44) **0116 234 0205**

THE HOUSE OF THE GOAT

Gerald Verner

Investigating the murder of a shabby man who had asked directions to the home of Lord Lancroft before being found brutally stabbed, Superintendent Budd has only one clue. Inside the man's jacket is a piece of paper, on which is written the Lord's name and address, and the words 'The House of the Goat' . . . And when an ancient mummy is stolen in the search for a mysterious ring, nothing is as it seems . . .

CODE OF SILENCE

Arlette Lees

When Sterling Seabright is found strangled
in the woods outside the small farming
community of Abundance, Wisconsin,
even her closest friends are shocked to
learn of her secret life. When a second
body is found murdered in a cabin by
the lake, it's up to Deputies Robely
Danner and Frack Tilsley to discover
the link. Sterling's classmates hold vari-
ous pieces of the puzzle, and although
they may be talking among themselves,
Robely and Frack are unable to break
their code of silence..